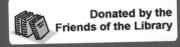

the dead I know

SCOT GARDNER

HOUGHTON MIFFLIN HARCOURT
BOSTON   NEW YORK

www.hmhco.com

Text set in Bembo Std

Library of Congress Cataloging-in-Publication Data
Gardner, Scot.
The dead I know / by Scot Gardner.
p. cm.
Originally published in Australia by Allen & Unwin in 2011.
Summary: Aaron Rowe's new job at a funeral parlor may be his salvation
from sleepwalking, dreams he cannot explain, and memories he cannot
recover, but if he does not discover the truth about his hidden past
soon, he may fall asleep one night and never wake up.
ISBN 978-0-544-23274-7
[1. Sleepwalking—Fiction. 2. Funeral homes—Fiction. 3. Dreams—Fiction.
4. Memories—Fiction. 5. Emotional problems—Fiction.] I. Title.
PZ7.G179336De 2015
[Fic]—dc23
2013050162

Manufactured in the United States of America
DOC 10 9 8 7 6 5 4 3 2 1

4500516247

1

THE OFFICE OF JKB FUNERALS was a majestic orange-brick addition to a modest orange-brick house. It had the boxy gabled ends of an old chapel with tall narrow eyes of stained glass to suit. There were concrete urns on either side of the entry door, spilling with white flowers. I checked my front for breakfast crumbs and then rapped on the door.

It opened with the smoothness of automation, but there was a man at the handle, a round man with half a smile on his easy, ruddy face. He looked me up and down, then shielded his eyes as if my head were at the top of a distant mountain.

"You must be Aaron," he said. "Please, come in."

I wiped my feet more than necessary, and stepped past the man into the cool silence of the building. The door hushed shut, and he held out his hand.

"John Barton."

We shook. It was a strange sensation. I'd never shaken hands with anybody.

"Please, come through. Have a seat."

The chairs were deep, lugubrious leather—more comfortable than anything I'd ever sat in.

"Thank you for coming in, Aaron. Your school counselor speaks very highly of you. I'm proposing a three-month trial period, at the end of which we'll sit here again and assess how we've gone. The work you'll be doing will be varied. There'll be some fetching, heavy lifting, and cleaning. Is your back okay? Need a good back in this line of work."

I nodded.

"Good. Now . . . appearance. Do you have a black suit?"

I shook my head.

He snatched a pen from a plastic holder and made notes on a pad. "No matter. I'll have Mrs. Barton measure you up, and we'll get something tailored."

"I have a black tracksuit," I said.

John Barton looked up, startled. "Tracksuit? No, I mean dress suit. What size shirt are you?"

I shrugged. "XL?"

He wrote some more. "You have an accent, Aaron. Where are you from? America?"

I shrugged again. "I grew up here."

"Is that so? What are your parents' names? I may know them."

"I doubt it," I said.

The words hung in the air like a balled fist. John Barton dug no deeper.

"Right," he said. "First things first. How would you feel about getting a haircut?"

One more shrug. "Fine."

"The first one is my treat."

John Barton gave me a fleeting tour—office; chapel and viewing room with visitors' bathrooms between them; display room; storeroom full of plastic-wrapped coffins standing on their ends; cool-room door—on our way to the garage at the rear of the establishment. There was a quietness and studied neatness to the whole place. The service areas smelled of flowery air freshener, with a metallic underscore of disinfectant. The garage, on the other hand, smelled of cool oiled dust. There were three vehicles parked inside—a fine silver Mercedes sedan, a white van that looked like an unmarked ambulance, and the hearse. The hearse's chrome and black luster rendered it catlike and serious in the glow from the skylight. There was a discreet crest painted on the driver's door containing three curlicue letters: *JKB*. The customized number plates echoed the starkness of the hearse's exterior—THEEND. If I'd been alone, I might have smiled at that.

"We'll take the Merc. Do you have a license?"

I shook my head.

"We'll have to do something about that."

It was a smooth ride, scented with leather and more air-freshener flowers. John Barton drove with an easy poise, as if he operated at a more precise speed than the rest of the world. He double-parked on Chatswood, in front of the barber's red and white spiral pole.

"The proprietor is Tony Henderson. Tell him I'll be paying. I'll be back in twenty minutes."

I nodded once and slipped out of the car. The door shut with a quiet huff of air, and I felt . . . something. Hard to say what it was—some gray wake of a distant emotion, perhaps.

It was early in a barber's day, but the floor already boasted small piles of gray and brown hair. Tony Henderson nodded a greeting.

"John Barton will pay," I said.

He ushered me to a chair.

"How would you like it?"

"Funeral director."

He chuckled. "Enough said."

He touched my head and I flinched.

"Sorry," he said, and then looked at his hand. "Okay?"

I nodded and clenched my jaw. I hadn't planned to flinch.

I noticed his aftershave and the dark hair on his knuckles. I avoided the mirror by staring at my cloaked knees as great long hanks of hair skidded over the smock and onto the floor. I tried to remember my last haircut and could think only of a time in fifth grade when I had been forced to remove a wad of gum from my hair with scissors. It was Westy—one of the drunks now living in caravan fifty-seven—who put it there, and he'd squealed with laughter when it stuck.

Tony Henderson shifted my head this way and that. He lifted my chin, but stood between the mirror and me as he did so.

"A shave?" he asked.

A nod.

Foam and a brush that had seen better days. Sharp steel in a practiced hand. I could see my shape in the mirror, but I didn't let my eyes focus.

Tony Henderson stood back and admired his handiwork. "I think you'll pass."

As if on cue, the bell on the door tinkled, and John Barton entered.

"Morning, Tony. I sent my new lad in here earlier. Did you see . . ."

Tony Henderson spun my chair, unclipped my smock, and dusted my neck and face with a soft brush. I waded through the clippings on the floor. I avoided the mirror and, in doing so, looked straight at my new employer.

He was smiling and shaking his head. "Are you sure it's the same fellow?"

Tony Henderson seemed pleased with himself. "Who'd have thought, hey? Tall, dark, *and* handsome."

"With the emphasis on dark," John Barton added, not unkindly.

"True," Tony Henderson said. "That's a bonus in your industry, isn't it?"

"Indeed."

John Barton drew his wallet from his pocket and laid a fresh fifty on the counter. He patted it and turned to leave. "Keep the change."

"Very kind of you, John. Thank you."

"No, thank *you,* Maestro. Thank you."

2

JOHN BARTON HAD BOUGHT two white dress shirts, and he handed me the bag as the garage door whined shut behind us.

"Come," he said, and I followed him through a side door into a small grassy garden between the office and the residence. A clothesline full of white shirts and incongruously bright silk boxers creaked idly in one corner. John Barton caught me staring.

"Yes, they're my shorts. The suits are always black, but I'm happy underneath."

Too much information, I thought. *I mean, underpants pride?*

A disheveled ginger cat mewed a mournful greeting as we passed. John Barton mumbled a reply and bent to rough its head.

"Morning, Moggy," he said. "This is Aaron. Aaron, this is Moggy."

"I . . . um . . . Good morning, Moggy," I said. I gave the cat a quick pat on the back.

John Barton smiled. "She's an oldie but a goodie. Just recently she's decided that the whole house is her litter box. Pays to wear slippers in the morning."

The house was full of television—all blue, blinking fury and noise. John Barton found the remote and poked it until the commercials became conversational.

"Dearest?" he called.

"In here," came the reply.

"We have a visitor."

The woman who walked into the room wore a peach apron over a floral nightmare of a dress. Her hair was gray and limp like Mam's. She grinned to reveal crooked teeth and shook my hand with enthusiasm, her fingers cool and soft.

"Goodness, you're a tall one!"

"Aaron Rowe, Delia Barton. Mrs. Barton to you."

"Oh, please call me Delia," Mrs. Barton said.

"Respect where respect is due, dear."

"Don't be so stuffy! Cup of tea?"

"Yes, please," John Barton answered. "Any messages?"

Mrs. Barton swished off to the kitchen. "Mrs. Gray is ready to be collected."

John Barton sighed. "At rest at last."

A stillness settled over the room. Were they speaking about a death? Was Mrs. Gray being collected from the mall with her shopping, or pried from a car wreck on the highway?

"Could you measure Aaron, my dear?" John Barton called. "He needs a suit."

"Of course!" his wife replied.

John Barton inspected a scrap of paper beside the phone. "Best put one of those shirts on," he said. "There's a bathroom just along the hall."

I closed the bathroom door behind me quietly. A hairy

brush rested in the sink. There was no room for it on the bench with all the beauty products and pill bottles. A wet mat was bunched on the floor beside a pile of discarded teddy-bear pajamas and underwear. The air was all talcum, wet towels, and fake flowers.

And there, in the mirror, was a stranger I had once known. His face was longer and leaner than I remembered, his skin smooth and clean. His black hair fell to the brow above the eyes it used to conceal. He had ears—two—and a new jawline.

"Sorry about the mess in there," Mrs. Barton called.

Her voice shattered my reverie, and I hurriedly tore open a shirt packet.

"We have a small piglet who lives with us. We call her Skye."

The stiff, clean cotton felt rich on my skin. It was a good fit, and I tangled with the buttons until there was no doubt about who was wearing whom. I undid my heavy belt and tucked the tails away inside my black jeans. I'd never worn white. I screwed the packet into a ball, but it wouldn't fit in the bin overflowing with tissues and empty toilet rolls. I carried it back into the lounge.

Mrs. Barton whisked it from my fingers and looked me over.

"Ah," John Barton said. "Now we're getting somewhere." He tapped his chin with an index finger, then departed.

Mrs. Barton held up a tape. "Measurements." She smiled and stretched her arms wide like a scarecrow.

I imitated her, and she fluttered over me, mumbling and penning numbers on a pad she pulled from her apron pocket.

When John Barton returned, he carried a sash of deep green silk. He draped it over my outstretched arm. A necktie.

"Right," Mrs. Barton said. "That's you done."

"Thank you, my dear," John Barton said. "Could you arrange for Tommy So to make one jacket and two pairs of pants?"

I felt the heavy silk of the tie between my fingers. It was suddenly all too much: the haircut, the shirts, and the suit. I had no idea how to knot a tie.

"Here," Mrs. Barton said, and snatched the tie. "Do up your top button."

"You've done enough," I said, and she stopped.

The television fell quiet and amplified the hole in the air I'd made. They stared.

"Nonsense," John Barton grumbled. "We've only just begun."

I looked at my shirt.

"If you were starting work at McDonald's, you'd need a silly uniform and one of those delightful hairnets. Think of the tie as our hairnet, and let Mrs. Barton put it on for you. She's the best in the business."

He smoothed his own tie, and Mrs. Barton tittered.

"Bend down," she said.

I lowered myself to one knee, and she tied the flat silken band around my neck. I felt like a character in a fairy tale.

"There you are," she said, and patted my shoulder.

I stood and stroked the tie. Embroidered in thread of the same green were three florid letters: *JKB*.

"Now, to work," John Barton said.

The cup of tea would have to wait, it seemed.

3

THE VAN WAS A MERCEDES as well, though it felt nothing like the ride in the sedan. John Barton drove at a measured pace.

"We'll be collecting the body of the late Mrs. Carmel Gray from Claremont. You know the place?"

He didn't wait for an answer. "All I need you to do is be silent and do as you're told. Do you understand?"

I gave a military nod, and he smiled dryly.

The breeze through the window whipped against my neck. In a curious way, I felt unburdened by the lack of hair. Something stirred in the pit of my belly, and I wondered if the late Mrs. Carmel Gray would like my shirt and my JKB tie and my new haircut. I wondered if I would be in the same room as the body. I wondered if I would smell the dead. Touch the dead.

Be silent. Do as you're told.

Claremont had a tradesmen's entrance, and John Barton had a key to the gate. He rattled the lock and tweaked the catch as if he'd done it a hundred times before. Thinking about it, I could see that carrying the dead through the automatic doors at the front would hardly be a good advertisement for an old people's home. The van beeped like a delivery truck as he reversed to the ramp.

A lady in uniform propped the doors open and offered us a tired grin.

"Morning, John," she said.

"The lovely Nina," John Barton replied.

"You've got a new lad?" Nina said, looking me over.

John Barton huffed. "Very perceptive of you, Nina. This is Aaron Rowe. Nina Cartwright."

She nodded approvingly. "Looks a whole lot better than the last one."

"Wouldn't have thought so this morning. Took a bit of cut and polish."

I stood by, listening to sparrows fighting in the hedge along the fence, as John Barton unloaded a trolley from the back of the van. Its legs unfolded automatically, dropping wheels smoothly onto the concrete path.

"What happened to Taylor?" Nina Cartwright asked.

John Barton cleared his throat, suddenly awkward. "He moved."

"Bound to happen, I suppose. Someone took out a contract on him then?"

He barked a laugh. "Nothing would surprise me."

He motioned for me to hold the trolley, and together we wheeled it through the doors and into the dim corridor. The smell was strangely familiar—musty and human. My ears strained to hold the frenetic chitter of the sparrows—there was something unsettling about the quiet inside the building.

There was no industry or hubbub, just numb silence. Nina whisked past, her stockings rubbing softly.

"Room thirty-seven," she whispered.

A screen had been erected around Mrs. Carmel Gray's cot. John Barton wheeled the trolley right into the room and asked me to shut the door.

I inhaled through my mouth, and I could taste the air. Talcum. Morning breath. John Barton held one end of the screen and, with a nod, instructed me to take the other. He counted, we lifted, and there was the late Mrs. Carmel Gray—arms holding the bedcovers to her sides, fingers cupped, and mouth frozen midyawn.

I sighed through my nose. This was death? This was what the world feared? I chuckled. It passed my lips as a hiccup.

John Barton shot me a questioning glance. "Are you okay?"

I nodded and left my head bowed.

I hadn't laughed at Mrs. Carmel Gray. I hadn't laughed at her unseemly gape or her partly lidded stare. It was the irony that caught me off-guard; almost every person alive feared Death, a commanding cloaked figure wielding a sickle, yet here death was a casual, sleepy release.

"Mrs. Gray won't be needing the blanket anymore, will you, dear?" John Barton said. "Aaron will help you with that."

He caught my eye and nodded. Without thinking, I held Mrs. Carmel Gray's gelid fingers and lifted her arm so I could draw the covering away.

"Leave the sheet," John Barton murmured.

I folded the blanket and placed it on a chair.

John Barton began untucking the sheet below Mrs. Carmel

Gray, and I did the same on the other side. He drew the top sheet over Mrs. Carmel Gray's head without pause or apology, stood at the top of the bed, and motioned for me to take my place at her feet.

"Take the lower sheet," he said, and screwed a fistful of it with each hand.

He counted, we lifted, and the late Mrs. Carmel Gray moaned a single drawn-out note. A mishandled accordion noise.

My body chilled and I almost dropped her.

"Hush, dear," John Barton admonished. "We're taking you home."

Her legs landed heavily on the trolley, and her body bent.

"Lift again," John Barton said. "Straighten her up."

I did as I was told.

John Barton tucked her arms under the top sheet and strapped her on — chest and thighs — for the ride.

"Get the door."

I did as I was told.

Nina Cartwright was waiting outside. She looked along the hall and ushered us out. There was nobody else there to witness our departure. Smoothly, almost without noise, we wheeled the trolley through the double doors and to the back of the van.

"Stand clear," John Barton said.

I let the trolley roll. The wheels and legs folded as the van swallowed the late Mrs. Carmel Gray. John Barton closed the doors quietly and nodded goodbye to Nina.

"Close the gate," he said to me.

John Barton's driving was even more composed on our way back to the office. The traffic hooted and bustled around us, but the rush was lost on John Barton.

"Ninety percent of our work is like that," he said to the windscreen. "A quiet end to a long life well lived. The dead don't put up much of a fight, and we're never in a hurry. Mostly, the families of our clients are both happy and sad to see us. Sometimes emotions run high."

He beeped the van backwards into the garage, leaving the doors open, and killed the engine.

"Now, I'll get you started on the hearse, and I'll take Mrs. Gray inside. Have you washed and polished a car before?"

I wanted to say yes. I'd seen it done.

"Fine," he said. "It may take a few tries to get it right, but we won't need it for a couple of days."

Loaded with a hose, a bucket of warm water, a sponge, and a complete arsenal of washing and polishing agents, I was set to work on the car. John Barton parked it on a patch of shaded grass and explained exactly what he wanted, once and clearly.

"I don't want to see a single spot, streak, or smear of polish. Do a little bit at a time until you can see yourself in every panel. Understand?"

My nod was more of a bow this time.

I washed and dried and polished for more than an hour. Around midday a group of kids—in the same school uniform I'd been wearing myself three days ago—made their way along the street. Off on an illicit lunch excursion to town, I suspected. I moved to the other side of the car as they drew close, but they decided to cross and walked right behind me. One boy was from my class. My pulse quickened.

"Nice car," he said.

One of the girls laughed.

"Shut up," he said. "It's a beast."

"What is THEEND supposed to mean?" the girl asked.

"You *are* joking!" the boy said.

Damien van Something. I caught his eye. I held his gaze for a full second.

He nodded coolly and they walked on.

It seemed I was unrecognizable already.

There was a peaceful rhythm to the cleaning and polishing. I was unrecognizable to myself.

Here was a task with boundaries and purpose, a small thing that made sense. A small thing I could do well.

Again, I felt something. A change in the weather, a shift in the season, something dawning or something setting. Some tide on the move or moon made full. Stirrings of ancient dust.

John Barton had his sleeves rolled up when he returned. He wiped his hands on a clean white cloth and made a circuit of the hearse. At one point he stooped and squinted but didn't touch the car.

He finished his lap toe to toe with me. He examined my eyes. I held his gaze, though I couldn't breathe.

"You are an enigma, young man," he said.

I didn't know how to respond, but I didn't have to. He patted my shoulder. Once.

4

MRS. BARTON HAD MADE a substantial plate of pale sandwich fingers: cheese and pickles, egg and lettuce, ham and more cheese. All the crusts had been sawn off, and they were embarrassingly easy to eat. I stopped when I realized she was watching me.

"Eat!" she said. "They'll only go to waste."

I ate one more. I could have emptied the plate.

The phone rang three times while we had lunch. John Barton answered each call, and I found myself staring at the back of his head, listening to his conversation, imagining the person on the other side.

Mrs. Barton stepped between her husband and me. "So, do you live in town, Aaron?"

I nodded.

She was waiting for more detail. I ignored the invitation.

"Where?" she finally asked.

I drew a line with my finger, through their garage and off toward the beach.

"By the water?"

I nodded again.

"How lovely! Have you been there long?"

One more nod. John Barton hung up the phone.

"I see," Mrs. Barton said. "Live with your mother and father?"

"Oh, leave the boy alone, dear," John Barton said. "He doesn't need the full twenty questions now. Besides, we have work to do."

He collected his jacket, and I took it as my cue.

"Bathroom," he said. He pointed to the bathroom where I'd changed earlier. It was hard to believe it was the same day. I used the toilet—not because I had to but because I was doing as I was told—and found John Barton reversing the hearse into the garage. We were in the van and out the door without exchanging another word.

He stuck a note to the dash. "The late Mr. Neville Cooper," he said. "Botany Street, number thirty-four. With a pickup from a private residence, we should be a little more cautious. We'll be discreet and park as close to the house as we can. We have to plan a route with the gurney and consider door widths, the size and weight of the body, family members, and the general public. You won't need to worry about any of that. Same rules: be silent and do as you are told."

Mr. Neville Cooper was a big man who had died in his bed. His three daughters sat, red cheeked, with their mother in the living room. I remembered the eldest one from my first high school, though I couldn't recall her name. She was a year or two older than I and had long, deep-red hair that made you take a second look.

In the passage, John Barton spoke with a nurse in hushed tones.

"One hundred and seventy kilograms," the nurse wheezed. "And don't I know it."

John Barton sized up the bedroom doorway and the hall. The front entry involved six concrete stairs; the rear, a single step onto rough paving, and a steep slope down the driveway.

"Back door," John Barton said to me. "Get the gurney."

I did as I was told. It took me a full minute to find the Velcro straps that held it in the van. The legs extended for me as they had for John Barton, and it rattled like an errant shopping cart over the bricks to the back stairs. With a push and a lift, the gurney nudged at the screen door. One hand on the door and one tugging the trolley, I broached the threshold and slid quietly through the laundry and kitchen to the bedroom.

The late Mr. Neville Cooper was a mountain of stomach under a blue sheet. Hospital machines stood mutely in the corner of the room. The gurney was higher than the bed, and John Barton adjusted it until they were level.

"Team lift," John Barton whispered.

"Might I suggest a roll?" the nurse said.

"Very good idea," John Barton said, and we assembled on one side.

The nurse began untucking the sheet below the big man, and I took my place beside her and helped. Two fistfuls of blue sheet each, and we were ready.

John Barton counted and we lifted. The body barely moved. John Barton counted again, and this time we heaved with a combined force that pitched the late Mr. Neville Cooper onto his side, onto the gurney, and then—with a crunching, fleshy slap—onto the floor beyond.

The nurse swore. She stepped across the room and closed the door.

The late Mr. Neville Cooper had been naked under the sheets and now lay sprawled on the floorboards, his backside dirty, proud, and parted. John Barton quickly covered the man's bruised skin with the sheet and held his own mouth and nose. The smell hit me at that moment—sick man's feces and decay—and my body lurched involuntarily.

"Come on, boys," the nurse growled. "Show a bit of stomach."

John Barton nodded and let his mouth go. "Oh, it's not the smell."

The nurse lifted the sheet clear and arranged it on the floor beside the body. John Barton apologized to the dead man under his breath. He lowered the trolley almost to the floor.

"Team lift?" he said.

"Great idea," the nurse whispered.

We rolled the late Mr. Neville Cooper onto the sheet and with a Herculean, knee-shaking effort moved his legs and then his torso onto the trolley. The nurse was strong and resolute. I needed to wash my hands but discreetly wiped them on the sheet instead. With the three of us lifting again, we got the trolley back up to full height. John Barton's brow was beaded with perspiration. He tugged and pushed until the body held a dignified symmetry on the stretcher, drew the sheet over Mr. Neville Cooper's head, and strapped him on. Tight.

"We'll take it easy. Just one step at a time," John Barton said, puffing. "Is the back of the van open?"

I nodded.

"Get the door."

I smoothed my tie, shook the nonexistent hair off my face, and opened the door.

One of the gurney wheels squeaked a mournful rhythm. I steered. John Barton pushed. The late Mr. Neville Cooper buffed the doorjambs with his shoulders. The nurse slipped past and opened the screen door.

That single step looked like the Grand Canyon. Beside me, the nurse grabbed the trolley, and we inched the wheels to the edge. John Barton used his entire weight to slow the descent—I heard his shoes rasping on the concrete. Suddenly, the gurney passed the point of no return and thunked to the paving. It landed unevenly and teetered. The nurse gasped. I heaved, and the wheel came back to ground. The rear wheels followed with an excruciating crash, and John Barton lost his footing. We were all dragged six meters by the quivering mass of the late Mr. Neville Cooper until John Barton found his feet and applied them as brakes. We slowed, but the body on the gurney didn't stop—merely continued its inexorable grind toward the van, with us towed behind. The nurse bailed, and I gave one last shove as the wild thing banged into the bumper of the van. Dead on target. The legs and wheels folded with an indignant clatter, and the late Mr. Neville Cooper came to rest in the back of the van with a hollow *gong*.

John Barton didn't let go immediately. He held tight as the rocking of the van eased. He relaxed his grip slowly but surely and dusted his hands a little theatrically.

The nurse smiled.

"Thank you," he said.

She dipped her head.

"Thank you both."

I met his gaze.

He blew air at his bangs and grinned. "I'll get some particulars. You can wait here if you like."

The nurse chose to wait with me.

I closed the doors of the van, and she leaned against them beside me.

"I don't envy you your job."

"I wouldn't swap it for yours," I said.

She stared at me with that questioning look people often get when I open my mouth. She stuck out her hand. "Sarah French, by the way."

"Aaron Rowe," I said, and shook her fingers.

"Been working with Mr. Barton for long?"

"My first day," I said.

Her jaw dropped. "How's it going?"

My words dried up. I'd already used more than my daily quota, and the dull ache in my head was a warning not to overdo it. I shrugged.

She waited for me to elaborate, and when nothing was forthcoming, she crossed her arms.

"He's a good man, Mr. Barton. He's done all my family funerals. And a few friends'. I wouldn't go to that other crew even if . . . even if I were dead!"

She laughed at her own joke.

"Selkirk Brothers is a factory. Pour dead bodies in one end; get ashes or a plot out the other. I see them all the time, rubbing their hands together over the dead and their loved ones.

The more grief, the better for them. Means a better sale. Vultures."

She shivered.

"Mr. Barton isn't like that. He didn't even charge my aunty when my niece drowned. Beautiful service with flowers and everything, and he didn't charge her a cent."

A minute passed. Sarah French watched the breeze lazily flipping the leaves on a tall poplar at the back of the yard.

"Oh well, that's me done. Better go and pack up my gear before the van gets here. Nice to meet you, Aaron. Good luck with your new job."

I mouthed "Thank you," and she was gone, up the back step and into the house. I climbed into the passenger seat and could smell the late Mr. Neville Cooper—all swampy and unflushed—and almost climbed back out again, but Sarah French's words were wafting around in there, too: "Show a bit of stomach." It was no worse than the toilets at the caravan park, just complicated by the fact that the source of the smell was dead and it was never going to get any better. I wondered how bad the van would smell if the corpse to be collected was rotting. No amount of fake flowers would cover that.

5

THE ENGINE TICKED as it cooled. John Barton stared at the windscreen until the smell was too much.

"Time for your final bath, Mr. Cooper," he said.

It was a smooth transition from the van to the cool-room. I held the side of the trolley and steered but felt superfluous. The cool-room door gave a stagey creak as it opened. John Barton flicked a switch as we entered, and banks of bright tubes blinked to life, illuminating two corpses—an old man dressed in a suit and the late Mrs. Carmel Gray, covered to the neck with a deep-green sheet. There were three empty gurneys and a stainless steel bench over a drain in the floor. The air was fridge-cool but not frozen, sharp with disinfectant and hard to breathe.

"Thank you, Aaron. Might finally be time for that cup of tea," John Barton said, and I followed him into the house. The jabber of the TV came out to greet us.

Mrs. Barton made tea the way her husband drove—all poise and practical efficiency.

"Sugar, dear?" she asked.

I shook my head.

"Milk?"

"No, thank you."

"Ah, much better manners. I love it when you use your words. I can't hear your head rattling."

John Barton ushered me to a seat at the round kitchen table. Mrs. Barton slipped two cream-filled biscuits onto my saucer.

Something rubbed my leg. I pulled back, but the rubbing continued. I slid my chair out and revealed Moggy, wiping her face on my shin.

Mrs. Barton pressed her slippered foot into the animal's rear. "Leave him alone, Moggy."

The cat slunk into the living room.

"She's an affectionate animal," Mrs. Barton said. "There's no doubting that. Just wish she could keep her fishy dribble to herself."

I slid my chair back under the table.

"So, how's it all going, then?" Mrs. Barton asked.

"Very impressed," John Barton said, almost under his breath. "Young Aaron here is a natural. He keeps it up, and he'll make a fair funeral director one day."

I heard what he was saying. I understood why he said it. Everything was new. They didn't know me. Starting a new school had been the same—falsetto cheer and painted smiles for the first few days, and then, like my teachers, the Bartons would realize I wasn't being shy or reticent. I was being myself. Each new school was the beginning of a journey of sorts: from the shores of polite enthusiasm, through the vast plains where I was blissfully ignored, and eventually to the land of insults and contempt. It was safer to move than fight back. Five schools in as many years.

"That *does* sound promising," Mrs. Barton said.

The back door opened with a bang, and the three of us jumped.

A girl entered. Her backpack hit the door, then the wall. She wore the yellow polo shirt and baggy navy shorts of the Catholic primary school, and was eleven or twelve at a guess. Her blond hair, bound in two tight braids, curved to touch her shoulders. She kicked off her black leather shoes and shed her bag.

"Here she is," John Barton said. "Afternoon, Skye."

She froze when she noticed me. Stared.

"Hello, darling," Mrs. Barton said. "How was your day?"

She didn't answer.

I stared back.

"Skye," John Barton said. "This is Aaron Rowe."

Still she stared. She appeared to be reading me like a bus timetable.

"Skye?" Mrs. Barton said. "That's enough, dear. What would you like to eat?"

She showed no sign of having heard.

"Skye!" John Barton barked, and she jumped. The spell was broken, and we breathed again.

"When's Taylor coming back?" Skye asked.

Mrs. Barton tutted. "We've been through this a hundred times, Skye. He's moved. Gone. He's not coming back."

But Skye wasn't waiting for a response; she had found the

remote and flumped on the couch. She turned the volume up further and skipped across channels until John Barton growled and scraped his chair noisily on the floor.

Mrs. Barton glanced at me and shrugged apologetically.

John Barton looked at his watch. "That will do for today, Aaron. You are free to go. Would you like a lift anywhere? Where's home?"

"Down by the water," Mrs. Barton revealed.

"I see," John Barton said. "I could drop you home if—"

"No," I said.

John Barton smoothed his tie, nodded.

"Thank you," I added. "I like to walk."

6

MAM WASN'T HOME. I checked the laundry and listened from the men's to make sure she wasn't in the
toilet either. Her purse was missing, and I guessed she'd gone
to the supermarket, even though shopping day wasn't until
Wednesday. She wouldn't have any money before then. I knew
that for a fact.

I swapped my work shirt for a T-shirt and took the long
way out of the park to avoid van fifty-seven—they'd be wak-
ing up about now—then jogged and walked along the foreshore and into the supermarket.

Mam was at the checkout. She was digging in her purse.
The checkout girl had called the manager and was standing
beside the till with her arms crossed.

The manager had done this before. "Any more change in
there, Mrs. Rowe?"

I took the last twenty from my pocket and handed it to the
manager.

"Ah," the manager said. "Here's your knight in shining
armor."

"This is David," said Mam.

"Aaron."

"This is Aaron," said Mam. "Give us a hand with the shopping, love."

I gathered the bags and collected the change before taking Mam's elbow and leading her into the street.

As soon as we were outside, she shook me off and stopped to investigate the notices on the community board.

I inspected the bags—two large containers of dishwashing detergent, toilet paper, and an orange. I thought about going back inside and making an exchange, but thinking about it was as close as I got.

"Washing machine," Mam read. "One hundred dollars."

"That's a good price."

"Yes. Not bad. Not bad at all," Mam said, and continued walking down the street. "Better have a look at it first, though. Can't trust them."

I followed and contemplated how best to prepare our evening meal of dishwashing liquid and toilet paper. The orange would be halved for dessert; that much was obvious.

The pedestrian turnstile at the caravan park groaned as we entered. I steered Mam behind van fifty-seven—they were shouting at each other over the metal music. The television in our annex was already on. She lowered herself into her armchair.

"*Deal or No Deal? Deal or No Deal? Who Wants to Be a Millionaire?*" she asked.

"Yes, please," I said. Although becoming a hundredaire would be a vast improvement.

While putting the dishwashing liquid away under the sink, I

found two more full bottles. I put the orange in the fridge and found another half-empty bottle of detergent masquerading as a milk carton in the door. There was nowhere to put the toilet paper except the table.

Frozen chicken fillets thawed in the microwave. Pasta sauce of bacon, cream, and parmesan cheese. Penne. We both had seconds. I washed the dishes with the chilled detergent while she was over in the shower.

"Bedtime, David."

"Aaron."

"Bedtime, Aaron."

"Yes, Mam. Good night, Mam. Sleep well."

She was snoring before nine. The familiar noise rattled over the muted TV as I left.

When sleep is not a sanctuary, darkness sometimes is. When the mess of human activity nags at you, the ocean can make you deaf with its rhythmic wash. I kept my T-shirt on but buried my jeans, socks, and shoes in the warm sand. I waded into the water until the tide dragged at my shorts, then I dived, swallowed at once by the ocean's maw. I lay there on my back—heavens above, darkness below—feeling impossibly small and vulnerable.

I listened, but all I could hear was bubbles and sea creatures clicking. I listened so hard, I thought I could hear the sand moving, but it was only my breath. In time, the calm made it to my core, and I swam to the beach. I carried my clothes and shoes, roughed myself with a towel in the annex, and fell to my bed.

7

MY HEAD IS RINGING. *My attention lands on a curve beside a snarl of dirty bed sheet. I stop breathing, but I can't stop staring. The curve is slight, but in my dreamscape it seems monstrous. The curve is human, though the color is wrong. Then I see it for what it is: an arc of toenail painted orange.*

I woke, panting and ragged, on the floor of the annex. The green fiberglass panel in the ceiling bathed the scene in a surreal light. My palms were sweaty, and in my right fist I held the broken handle of a hairbrush, one I'd never seen before. Where had it come from? Had I broken it? I shook it from my palm and lifted myself to my knees, staring.

"Morning, Aaron," Mam said, startling me.

She stood in the door of the van with one hand on her hip.

"Morning."

"What you doing down there?"

"I . . . I was looking for the rest of my hairbrush," I said.

I collected the broken handle and my toiletries bag and made my way to the shower block. There were wrinkled feet in the second stall, but the shower wasn't running. I slipped the handle noiselessly into the trash can, then shaved and blasted my skin with the bleachy-smelling water. My hair, now so short, rebelled at my every attempt to calm it. In the end I let it have its own way and fled from the mirror.

Mam had made pancakes. I picked a piece from one and nibbled it ready to spit, but it was fine. Luscious, in fact. No soap flakes or laundry detergent. No talcum or hard cheese.

"Your hair looks nice, Aaron."

"Thank you."

"Did you cut it yourself?"

"No. Does it look like it?"

"A little. At the front. Mind you, you did a good job."

"Thanks."

If Mam were an alcoholic, her mental state would be easy to explain. If she'd taken drugs or had had an accident, her luck-of-the-draw world would make more sense. Sometimes she was lucid and practical; other times she was a stormy two-year-old. There was no rhyme or flow, just what she was served. Yet, for all her shifting states, she never woke with a stranger's broken hairbrush in her hand.

I couldn't knot my tie. It hung like a sash beneath my collar and across my chest. When John Barton met me at the door to his house, he stripped it from my neck and hung it over his own. He knotted it deftly as he escorted me into the cool-room, then loosened it and slipped it over his head.

"Can't tie them on anyone else," he said, and handed me the knot. "Slip it on and tighten it up."

I did the best I could.

John Barton made the final adjustments and brusquely flattened my collar over the top.

"You'll do," he said. He lifted a pile of green fabric and handed it to me. "Your apron, mask, glasses, and gloves. Get them on. We have work to do."

I sat the pile on an empty gurney and sorted my way into them. The old man in the suit had gone. Mrs. Carmel Gray was dressed. The mountain of Mr. Neville Cooper was now under green cotton, his toes protruding. My dream returned as a chill down my spine.

"It's not a hospital, but we have to be clean. Some people die from disease, and those diseases may be transmissible from their remains. Viral infections, AIDS, hepatitis B. To be on the safe side, we avoid contact with blood, feces, and mucus where we can. We'll wear gloves."

I stood there, more surgeon than undertaker, and John Barton adjusted my protective clothing until he was satisfied.

"After you left last night I gave Mr. Cooper a wash. He'll need to be dressed this morning. Mrs. Gray is being cremated this afternoon and she needs a box."

I heard what he was saying, but I couldn't drag my eyes from the toes. The more I stared, the more my dream returned. There was no nail polish, but the real and the dream merged; Mr. Neville Cooper's toe was dead, and the toe in the dream was dead. That much I knew.

John Barton was watching me when I escaped from the trance.

"You okay?"

I nodded.

"It's quite acceptable to be a little confused or confronted by this. I mean, it takes a bit of—"

"It's nothing," I said.

John Barton stiffened, then shrugged. "You'll find a black suit bag hanging behind the door in my office. Bring it in."

I did as I was told. He directed me to a hook on the wall of the cool-room and instructed me to unzip the bag.

"Shoes out. Socks out," John Barton said. "Is there any underwear in there?"

Boxer shorts, as lurid as the ones on John Barton's clothesline.

"Excellent."

He stripped the green sheet off the body, folded it roughly, and pitched it across the room at a basket. He scored and seemed pleased by the shot.

"Right, over here," he called.

I joined him at Mr. Neville Cooper's feet. With the sheet removed, the body didn't echo the dream. He was a dead thing again. A shell.

"Take a foot," he said.

I didn't hesitate. The skin was cold but still supple, the surface smooth.

"Lift the leg. He's a bit stiff now, but we'll stretch him out and get him dressed together."

There was an intimacy about the process that caught me off-guard. Mr. Neville Cooper's genitals were concealed beneath the rolls of his stomach and thighs. His nakedness was incidental, like that of a pensioner dressing outside his shower stall at the caravan park. It was natural to look without seeing, and dressing him felt like an act of kindness—a helping hand for a fellow who couldn't help himself. Had Mr. Neville

Cooper been alive, the closeness would have been impossible. Dead, Mr. Neville Cooper was a safe friend.

His suit was spotless, perhaps new. John Barton coached me through the lifting and the yoga of loosening and dressing the dead, how to save your own back and balance while tucking and rolling. His movements seemed rough to begin with, but I later realized they were merely practical. He spoke as a tailor might, including the dead man in his mumblings.

"Now your left arm, Mr. Cooper. Nice big stretch. Good. A fine shirt they've chosen. Hand me the jacket and tie, Aaron."

We dressed Mr. Neville Cooper in his jacket, but John Barton left the top button of the shirt open and slipped the tie over his own head. He fussed with the sleeves and seams, and I stood back to appreciate the transformation. With the dignity conferred by the suit, it was possible to overlook Mr. Neville Cooper's wan features and imagine he was asleep.

John Barton drew the gurney carrying Mrs. Carmel Gray alongside so their heads were side by side.

They were tanning together in their fineries. It's possible I smiled at that thought.

A hospital tray carrying a single pump pack of vitamin E skin cream was rolled to a working distance, and I was ordered to stand beside Mr. Neville Cooper's resplendent remains.

"Do exactly as I do. Watch closely."

He took a squirt of cream and lathered it in his palms. He rubbed it on the back of Mrs. Carmel Gray's hand. I did the same for Mr. Neville Cooper. Beauty therapy for the dead.

"Try not to get it on the clothes. Take your time. Hands, face, neck, hairline. Any exposed skin."

John Barton nodded his satisfaction at my work. He buttoned the rest of Mr. Neville Cooper's shirt and knotted the tie around his own neck — as he'd done for me. He slid it in place and folded the collar expertly, then smoothed the dead man's hair as he might his own.

He handed me a photo of Mr. Neville Cooper before his demise.

"What do you think?"

I stared at the image. It had been taken at a wedding. It was hard to accept the fact that the two-dimensional picture in my hand now had more signs of life than the man before me. He looked younger in death.

"Our job is to create a memory picture for those left behind," John Barton said. "Some places they pump the dead full of embalming fluid and paint their faces with makeup. To my eye that looks unnatural. We don't want to bring them back to life; we only want to give them dignity. I spend a lot of time getting the hair right."

I hadn't noticed. It was picture-perfect and wouldn't have happened by accident. I wondered how much vitamin E cream he'd use on a car accident victim or those with their heads blown off by shotgun blasts. I wondered but I didn't ask.

"Mrs. Gray will be delivered in a Crenmore coffin. An Eternity model. Come," he said, and led me to the storeroom. "We keep about twenty caskets in stock and can get them here overnight when it's a special order. The names are on the packing labels."

We carried the Crenmore Eternity into the cool-room and positioned it on a lowered gurney. The plastic covering was dispatched with scissors so sharp, they needed no cutting action. For transport, the upturned lid had been screwed to the base.

"Use this," John Barton said, handing me a battery drill. "Take care not to scratch the finish. The lid is in two parts. You'll find hinges, handles, and screws to fit them inside. Bit of tab A goes into slot B. Think you can handle that?"

I nodded.

"Need I have asked?" he mumbled to himself.

The hinges and holes for the handles were all predrilled. It took me ten minutes to put the coffin together.

John Barton dumped an armload of silky white fabric into the box. "Lining is attached with the staple gun."

He murmured instructions and stapled the lining in place.

"Mattress," he said.

I thought he was joking. He wasn't. The coffin had a luxurious spring bed that we lowered into place.

Finished, it reeked of new paint and plastic, but I doubted Mrs. Carmel Gray would mind. With John Barton cradling her head and me lifting her sensibly shod feet, we lowered her in. The mattress springs creaked as they took her weight. Mrs. Carmel Gray's final bed felt more comfortable than the floor I'd woken on that morning. My dream from the dawn raced in and made me hold my breath. I blinked and shook the image of the orange toenail from my thoughts, replaced it with the square-heeled shoes on the body in front of me. Utilitarian and, yes, dignified old ladies' shoes.

We retired to the house for morning tea around eleven, and on the way past the chapel, I caught a glimpse of a closed coffin and an insight into how hard John Barton worked while my eyes were elsewhere. I guessed this was the old man from the cool-room. John Barton had collected and prepared, lifted and clothed, made up and presented the body and coffin by himself. I felt superfluous and in awe, and then my place in this world became clear—he could do all those things by himself, sure, but my back and my hands could share the load. Mrs. Barton presented me with a package. Apparently, Tommy So had had a suit on the rack that needed very little alteration to fit me.

John Barton was suspicious. "Try it on, Aaron. Seeing is believing."

I discreetly kicked the wet towels deeper into Skye's bathroom so I could close the door. The fabric was silken and light—like boxer shorts without the bright color and shine. The loops on the pants were too narrow for my belt, but the rest of the suit fitted well. In the mirror, my transformation was almost complete.

John Barton produced a narrow black leather belt from his wardrobe but had to punch a new hole. Like scientists, he and his wife examined their creation. I slipped my hands into my pockets.

"Ah!" John Barton growled, waggling a finger. "Your hands enter your pockets only to fetch something."

He gestured that I should copy him—hands clasped behind his back, hands hanging by his side, hands clasped in front.

"Very good. If I see you with your hands in your pockets, it'll be your turn for a ride in the hearse. In the back!"

I chuckled. It caught me by surprise.

John Barton and his wife stood stock-still, as if they were equally surprised. I covered my mouth.

"That's quite enough of that, too," John Barton said. "There'll be no laughing in here."

His finger was waggling again, but something akin to a smile had messed with his funeral director's expression.

We drank tea, and I wasn't required to open my mouth except to drink or shovel food in.

Eventually, John Barton looked at his watch and stood. "Will you give us a hand with Mr. Dean's flowers, please, my dear? People will be arriving in about an hour."

My rib cage seemed to tighten around my heart. I should have known there would be people. I should have guessed that the suit was not just for my own amusement.

The garage floor between the vehicles was a brawl of color. Giant bunches of flowers—eleven in all—shamelessly lit up the gray concrete. Mrs. Barton took one arrangement, then stood beside the coffin, placing the others that John Barton and I carried in. The smell of real blooms, all sappy and green, overcame the ubiquitous scent of fake flowers.

John Barton tugged on my sleeve and beckoned me into the hall.

"Same rules," he said. "Be silent and do as you're told."

I nodded.

He dusted a white petal from my shoulder. "You'll be fine. Remember to keep breathing."

My job was to greet the mourners and hand them a copy of the service for the late Mr. Arthur Terrence Dean. I didn't do much greeting, but I did hand out the programs. The photocopied picture gave him the most evil-looking skin, and his mad-scientist glasses made the overall effect a bit cartoonish. The body in the coffin wore the same glasses.

The bereaved took their seats, and I stood at the back of the chapel, my damp hands clasped in front of me. I could see the backs of their heads, but they watched the celebrant at the lectern, above the coffin. Flamboyant in purple and green, he made the rotund John Barton look like a swimsuit model.

"We're here to bid our farewells to Arthur . . . Arty . . . Terrence Dean. To celebrate his life and lay him to rest."

Why was my own heart hammering so loudly? Could the tall man in the back row hear it?

It wasn't the still body that unmanned me. It wasn't the flowers or the solemnity of the occasion. It was the people. The seething sea of emotion that filled the room to the rafters. The reddened eyes and the quiet sniffles, the hands held tight. They were each marked with the disease—the unmistakable symptoms of grief—and the very air I breathed was infecting me.

I hung there like a tortured animal through the whole service, shivering when it got the better of me, feeling faint, and waiting for the final blow.

It came from a lady in the front row. It came as John Barton discreetly pressed a button in the wall beside me and the coffin sank out of sight. The woman sobbed. I felt the wall of the dam breaking, and I ran. I hit the door on the way out. I ran onto the street. I didn't stop running.

8

IT WAS THE DREAM. It was as if that roomful of people were all tearing at the sheet in my nightmare. They were going to uncover the foot, the leg, the body hidden there, and I didn't want to know, didn't want to think about any of it. I wanted to tuck it all back down and get on with my life. Perhaps I could concentrate my efforts in the cool-room? John Barton could teach me to dress the bodies, and I could be his man behind the scenes.

I ran all the way back to the van.

The annex smelled burned. There was blood on the floor. Slick, dark blood, its color distorted by the green light from the fiberglass panel in the ceiling.

"Mam?"

No answer.

More blood on the floor of the van. I sprinted to the shower block, straight into the women's bathrooms.

"Mam?"

"Aaron?"

She was in a cubicle. The door was locked. The air was rank.

"Are you okay?"

"Yes, I'm fine. I had a little accident."

"Open the door."

"I'm fine."

"Please open the door." The latch clicked.

She sat, fully clothed, on the toilet seat. In the harsh white light of the toilets, the blood on her hands was purple.

"What happened?"

"Little accident, that's all."

"What's that on your hands?"

"What does it look like?"

"The purple."

"Oh, beetroot juice. I couldn't find the . . . thingy. I used something else. Can't a person have a bit of privacy these days?"

"What the hell's going on in here?" came a harsh woman's voice.

I spun to see the toothless woman from van fifty-seven standing in the doorway of the women's toilets, armed with a towel and pink cosmetics bag.

"Mam's had an accident. I was just—"

"You were just getting the hell out of here, you pervert."

I ran back to the van. Smoke now billowed from the annex door. I ducked in and found a frying pan on high heat, the contents smoking and blackened beyond recognition. I flung it on the gravel outside, opened all the windows, and turned on the fan.

I stomped out to wait for the smoke to clear. The frying pan had warped. I could see purple in the half-moon of food that wasn't carbonized. Fried beetroot.

I sat on my bunk in the annex until the air in the van was

breathable. There was beetroot juice splashed everywhere. The butchered can sat in the sink next to the hammer and screwdriver she'd used to punch it open.

The can opener was in the top drawer, where it had lived since before I could remember.

I hung my jacket on the back of Mam's armchair and rolled up my sleeves. The cloth cleaned up the beetroot, but the sense that I'd narrowly averted disaster remained. I couldn't wipe out the knowledge that Mam was a danger to herself and that I wouldn't be able to keep a job if I couldn't leave her alone. She'd seemed so composed that morning. She'd been in her right mind; I'd been the one acting a little crazy.

"Oh hello, Aaron. Dinner's almost ready."

"How can you say that?"

She blinked. "Say what?"

"Dinner's not nearly ready. Dinner's in the rubbish bin outside."

"What's it doing out there?"

"It doesn't matter."

"It *does* matter. What's it doing out there?"

"I threw it out there. It was burning. Burned beetroot."

She sat slowly, holding her mouth. "What's happening, Aaron? I feel as though I'm losing my mind."

It wasn't until she said those words that I realized how far she'd gone. Those words were the real Mam. It had been so long since I'd heard her that I'd forgotten what she sounded like. She shook. She buried her face in her hands.

I stood and hugged her head. "You're okay, Mam. We're

okay. Just having a bit of a rough time, that's all. It'll pass. It always passes."

She nodded against my chest.

I wanted to say more—now that her radio was finally tuned in, I needed to make the most of it—but the words fizzed and burned before they were free. I could smell her. She smelled like Mr. Neville Cooper.

"Come on," I said. "We'll get your things together so you can have a shower."

"I'll be okay."

"Yes. Even better after a shower. Come on." She held my hand and I hoisted her up.

I hid in the laundry beside the bathroom while she showered. I could hear the water going. I heard her soaping up noisily. I heard her blow her nose. The water eventually stopped.

"How you feeling, Mam?"

"Hey? Fine. Who's that?"

"It's Aaron."

"Fine, Aaron."

"I have to go."

"Okay. Will you be back for dinner?"

"Yes. It's my turn to cook."

"Oh, that's right. That'll be great. What are we having again?"

"Surprise."

"You devil."

I couldn't let John Barton down. I didn't know whether

I'd be able to find words to explain what had happened in the chapel, but returning to the scene would have to count for something.

I heard voices in his office. I knocked on the door.

"Come in," John Barton said.

The three seats in the office were occupied. All eyes turned on me.

"Sorry," I said.

"No, Aaron, that's fine. Won't be long. Could you wait in the house, please? Mrs. Barton has gone shopping, but you're welcome to make yourself a cup of tea. I'll be in shortly."

I nodded, closed the door quietly, and did as I was told.

The cat mewed. I couldn't see it at first—it was tucked behind the curtain in the lounge. It stood and stretched and rubbed itself on my suit pants. I dusted the fluff off, then scruffed its head as John Barton had done. It dribbled and purred like a motor. The house was eerily empty without the TV blaring. I made tea and boldly switched the television on. I sat on the edge of the couch and transferred my cup from hand to hand as it got too hot to bear.

The back door clattered.

I slopped my tea but didn't leave my seat.

Skye. She dropped her bag and flashed her teeth as greeting. I flashed my teeth in reply.

We both looked to the cat.

"Where's Mum?"

"Shopping."

"Where's Dad?"

"In with people. He'll be back soon."

"Why do you sound like a robot?"

"Do I?"

"Yes, you sound like the remote-control robot I had when I was seven."

I shrugged.

"Where do you keep your batteries?"

I smiled.

"Don't answer that. I don't want to know."

I sipped my tea, burned my lip, and slopped some more.

"I know where you live," Skye said.

"Oh?"

She nodded curtly. "Caravan park."

I feigned nonchalance.

"My friend Steevie lives on the corner, and I saw you going home last night when we were picking her up for basketball training. Why do you live in a caravan park? Can't you afford a house? Don't your mum and dad work or something? Are you a drug user? Steevie says heaps of drug users live in the caravan park. You look like a drug user."

She came closer and patted the cat, then grabbed the remote and cranked up the volume. She flicked stations.

"You don't talk much. Why don't you talk? Are you shy? Say something."

I stared at my cup.

"Say something. Go on, dare you. Say um . . . say '*ABC Kids*.' No, say 'Sony television remote control.' Go."

I blew on the tea. My breath made a shallow dent in the liquid.

"See? See, you can't even say that. You're shy. And you're on drugs. I can tell by those dark circles around your eyes. That's from smoking cocaine. Do you make your own? Do you have a drug-making place at the caravan park? You know, with the little flame thing and the glass bottles and colored bubble stuff? I take drugs. I do! Here, I'll show you."

She took a strip of plastic-wrapped pills from her shorts. She opened her hand in front of my face, then stuffed them back in her pocket.

"See? Told you. How much? How much are you going to pay? They're real drugs. They're strong. Really strong. They hardly work on me because my body is used to them. One hundred bucks. Each pill. Come on. Pay up."

If Skye's intrusiveness was designed to get a reaction, it worked. I took a breath. "I live in the caravan park because that's where Mam and I have always lived. Mam was a university professor, but she's retired now. Some of the people who live in the park use drugs. Some of the people who live on this *street* use drugs. I'm shy sometimes, but mostly I don't like to waste words. I don't make or take drugs, and I certainly won't be buying any of your period-pain medication."

Blood filled her cheeks. She stomped past me and slammed her bedroom door. She shouted something. It was almost a squeal and completely unintelligible.

John Barton arrived laden with plastic shopping bags.

I hurried into the kitchen and emptied my cup in the sink.

"Could you give Mrs. Barton a hand, please, Aaron?" He pointed outside. "Then I think we need to have a chat."

Mrs. Barton was at the back of the silver sedan. I took the bags from her.

"Oh, it's you. Thank you, Aaron."

I put the bags on the kitchen bench with the others.

"Right," John Barton said. "Office."

I followed him, feeling more than a little uneasy. He ordered me into a chair and stared at me questioningly. There was no accusation or ill will in his eyes.

"What happened?"

"I wish I knew."

He took a sharp breath.

"I . . . I wish I knew *exactly*. All the people . . ."

"The people? What about the people?"

"The people. It was overwhelming. Somehow. When you pressed the button and the coffin sank into the bench, I wanted to . . ."

"You wanted to what?"

"I had to leave."

He rested his chin on his palm and contemplated the planner on his desk.

I felt that he was weighing up my future. I wanted to say more. I wanted him to know that caring for the dead fitted me like old leather gloves. I wanted to thank him for rescuing me from school, but the thoughts never flowered and my mouth stayed shut.

"There's no shame," John Barton said quietly. "Funerals are the place for letting it out. They're the last free-for-all in our society. Without them we would all turn to stone from unexpressed emotion."

He looked me in the eye. "If it happens again, you can retreat in here or the viewing room. Cool-room. Store. Take a minute, compose yourself, then do what you can. It *does* get easier, at some level, the more you do it. It gets easier when you've met and dealt with your own grief. It gets easier, but it'll probably never be easy."

After a moment, when all that had sunk in, I nodded. "I'm sorry."

"No need to apologize," he said. "You're not the first, and you won't be the last to leave early from one of my funerals!"

I smiled, but he was staring at me again.

"If you need to talk, Aaron, I have two good ears."

I nodded.

He glanced at his watch. "Give me a hand to place Mrs. Gray and her flowers, and we'll call it a day. Okay?"

We lifted the coffin from the gurney onto the ornate bench in the chapel.

"This," he said, patting the bench, "is a catafalque, and the button up the back starts the part of the ceremony called the committal. The final goodbye. Dry eyes are rare at that part of the ceremony."

Mam had cut an onion into rings. I saw it on the table and on the floor, and I could still smell it on her fingers as she cradled my face in her hands. She held me as if I'd been away to war.

"Are you staying for tea, Aaron?"

"Yes, Mam. My turn to cook."

"That's very kind of you, but I've already made dinner."

The burned and buckled frying pan was back. She picked it off the cold stove by the handle, then put it down again, puzzled.

"Ah, I know that music," I said. "Sounds like your favorite show is on. Why don't you put your feet up while I get dinner organized?"

Her eyes lit up. "You're a good son. Your wife is a lucky woman."

Hold on, don't skip all the good bits, I thought. *Don't dream me a life without the romance. Let me do the coloring in myself.*

9

THE TOENAIL BELONGS *to a body bunched beneath the sheet. The shade of the polish—somewhere between saffron and sunset—infects the rest of the image, taking it from a monochrome to a lurid color. The sheet is pink. The stains on the linen and the marks on the wall are red. The spots are teardrops, and they are crawling toward the floor.*

I woke mid-blench in the flat, predawn light. I sat up. I was on a rough wooden table. Seconds passed as I struggled to get breath in my body and identify my surroundings.

The camp kitchen.

Sometime during the night I'd relocated one hundred meters to the hard, oily bench where itinerants ate barbecued sausages. The cold had drilled right through me. I could barely feel my feet on the concrete, the damp grass, the gravel, the smooth tiles of the bathroom. I turned the shower on hard and stepped into the steam still dressed in my T-shirt and underwear.

Why now? Why had the dream found its claws now? Was it the proximity to death that had brought it to life? Was Mam's madness infecting me, or was this a new insanity of my own design?

Men came and went and fouled the air with their ablutions and their perfume. I stayed there until my skin glowed and the daylight struggling through the frosted windows won the battle with the fluorescent tubes on the ceiling. Until the images and rabid chatter in my head had grown soft and wrinkled. Until the hot water was all gone.

A father with his sleepy-eyed son in his arms was entering as I was leaving.

"You're wet," the boy said.

The man chuckled. "Sorry."

"You're right," I said, and shook my hair, spraying them both.

The man laughed properly and hurried inside. "We don't need a shower now, do we, Sam?"

Mam was still asleep. I dried and dressed, but both work shirts smelled sweaty. I used the last of the change from the piggy bank to put them through the washing machine and the dryer. I ironed one of them and put it on. I hung the other in the annex.

"Hello, David," Mam croaked.

"Aaron."

"Hello, Aaron," Mam croaked again.

I made us an egg on toast each, kissed her tousled curls, and scurried off to work.

◎ ◎ ◎

John Barton wore his shirt open-necked, and his hair was combed but damp.

"Had a pickup very early this morning. I slept in," he said, and my fluster suddenly didn't seem so out of place. Perhaps everybody had had a strange night?

I handed him my tie, but he handed it straight back.

"Do as I do."

I stood beside him and copied like a monkey. I butchered it on the first try, but the second—with a bit of friendly yanking and twisting by John Barton—looked passable.

John Barton opened the cool-room door and recoiled at the smell.

Mr. Neville Cooper had soiled himself. We donned our protective gear and undressed him. His shirt, pants, and underwear had been caught in the evil tide. Only his jacket could be saved.

I lost my breakfast in the sink. John Barton was there with his hand between my shoulder blades.

"Go and wait outside, Aaron. I'll finish here."

I took three steps toward the door; then the nurse's words were there in my head: *Show a bit of stomach.*

I hung Mr. Neville Cooper's jacket behind the door and collected the rank mess of other clothes, trying desperately not to breathe.

"In the sink," John Barton wheezed. "Pink disinfectant."

I used the nailbrush and retched some more, but eventually the steely smell of the disinfectant won over.

"When you can stand to be in the same room as the clothes, put them in a bag and run them down to Mrs. Anderson at the dry cleaners' three doors down. Let her know the viewing is this morning. She'll know what to do."

I did as I was told. The air inside the dry cleaners' was heavy with solvent, and, thankfully, Mrs. Anderson *did* know what to do.

"Come back in an hour," she said, a little too brightly. She pinched the bag between two fingers and carried it to the rear of the shop.

John Barton's night pickup had arrived in a black zippered bag.

"From the coroner," he explained, tugging the zipper. The air grew still as he revealed the body.

Her body: a woman in her twenties with the sort of air-brushed perfection that I thought existed only in magazines. Her lips were barely parted, as in the moment before a kiss. Her face was so clean and tanned that I caught myself staring and had to look away. There were scratches and small cuts around her shoulders. A black-stitched scar ran from between her breasts to the soft curve of her stomach. I stared at John Barton as we lifted her clear of the bag and onto a new gurney, and kept watching him until he'd covered her with a clean white towel.

He tenderly brushed a blond lock from her forehead. "A surfer found her caught in the rocks below Keeper's Point. Coroner said she'd drowned. Threw herself off the cliffs."

I swallowed, and it made an awkward noise. I knew the place. I knew the place where she'd died and the dark place she'd been in before she went there, but I had questions. Was it courage that made her take the last step, or weakness? Was it loss that walked her to the edge, or a search for freedom? I took her hand from beneath the towel. The skin was cool and soft. I held it for only a moment before awkwardness got the better of me, but in that moment I wanted to weep and shout, rage and cry.

"Such a waste," John Barton said.

The platitude grated. *Did you hear that, Skye?* I thought. *That's what happens when you don't watch what you say; you end up sounding trivial and insincere. Here was a moment that called for silence, and your father spoiled it with a cliché.*

"The family has requested a viewing, and I can completely understand why. She's absolutely beautiful, even in death."

John Barton observed and instructed as I washed the girl's hair. My hands moved clinically, but my breathing had no rhythm. I found another scar at the back of her head. It was concealed by hair but stretched from ear to ear.

"After an autopsy, your brain could end up in your bum," John Barton said. "Literally."

I looked at him and tried to smile.

I toweled her hair—it hung halfway to the floor—and John Barton sent me back to the dry cleaners' for Mr. Neville Cooper's clothes. By the time I returned, the rest of the girl's body had been washed and dried. I was thankful to be spared that task.

We dressed Mr. Cooper, and John Barton prayed aloud. "Dear God, grant this man some dignity in his final hours aboveground."

I constructed and carefully lined a Crenmore Imperial coffin while John Barton prayed aloud again. "Dearest merciful

God, make this coffin big enough." He measured the shoulders and found they would fit. He measured the hips, and they would fit. It was the mound of the stomach that had him worried. He busied himself in the toolbox and returned armed with a dangerous-looking needle attached to a tube.

He unbuttoned Mr. Neville Cooper's jacket and clean shirt. When the rounded skin of the gut was exposed, he flicked a switch and a noisy pump started.

"Trocar," he said, waving the needle. He drove it into the dead man's belly, and the tube instantly filled with bloody liquid. "Aspiration."

The needle dug around inside Mr. Neville Cooper, slurping and bubbling. It was macabre, this gratuitous mutilation of a corpse. Until that moment, John Barton had cherished the dead, treated them with friendly care and respect.

John Barton eventually stopped the pump. He tenderly bathed, dried, and patched the hole with tape, and Mr. Neville Cooper's shirt and jacket fitted better than they ever had. He carefully lathered and shaved the dead man's gray-stubbled face. After the labor of levering Mr. Neville Cooper into his coffin, we found that the lid closed cleanly. The aspiration had been a practical necessity, I decided. The man was dead, after all.

The girl's name was Amanda Creen. One of her eyes was open a slit, as if she were discreetly watching our every move. John Barton wiped her eyes with a paper towel, then parted the lids properly and dried her eyeballs. In death, her irises had relaxed and left her with the startled black stare of a wild animal. Owl eyes. John Barton tore small pieces of a paper towel and pressed them to the delicate surface. With the lids drawn over the top, the paper towel kept them closed.

I blow-dried her hair and wished I'd had a sister or cousin to learn from. I raked it with a broad-toothed comb until it shone and made up its own mind about which way it was going to hang. Dry, it withdrew into silken ringlets and became half its length. It was so vital and alien between my fingers—

"Okay, that's probably enough time on the hair," John Barton said abruptly.

I stood and my knees cracked.

"My word," he said. "Your knees sound like mine! How old did you say you were again?"

I smiled, a little guiltily.

"We won't have a photo for a couple of days, but it looks as though her hair knows best. Good work."

He threaded a large curved needle and sewed Amanda Creen's mouth shut. It was a swift, practiced action—through the inside of the bottom lip, up and in front of the top teeth, into the nasal cavity, and back into the roof of the mouth. With the two ends tied and the excess thread trimmed, her lips lost their kiss and instead pretended to sleep.

10

THAT AFTERNOON, the same celebrant wearing the same garish purple and green tent conducted Mr. Neville Cooper's service. I stood at the back of the chapel and distracted myself from the proceedings with thoughts of Amanda Creen. I imagined lives for her that made sense of her death—a broken heart, a broken mind, an accident, foul play—all the while being drawn back by the luster of Mr. Neville Cooper's eldest daughter's hair. The living and the dead.

"Now Neville's eldest daughter, Nadia, would like to say something on behalf of the family," the celebrant wheezed.

Nadia. I remembered her name. She arrived at the dais with a red nose and flushed cheeks, and I had to leave. I caught John Barton's eye, and he nodded solemnly.

I slipped through the door without making a sound and fought the urge to run. I shoved my hands in my pockets and just as quickly ripped them back out again. What if Amanda Creen's heart had broken after a loss like Nadia Cooper's? What if the same loss could drive Nadia Cooper to the edge? The thought of her fiery hair spilling onto the stainless steel gurney made the blood in my veins go cold. What if the sight of me leaving as she got up to speak was the final straw? The idea was stupid, but for some reason it took hold of me and almost propelled me back through the double doors and into the chapel. Mad. It was real and confusing enough to keep me anchored to that piece of floor for the duration of the service. The music started, the coffin was committed, and people began moving. I stood at attention like a guard, with my hands clasped in front of me, avoiding eye contact with the mourners as they left. All except one. The bloodshot eyes of Nadia Cooper caught mine. She was moving slowly, and she peered up at me with a broken smile.

"I'm . . . sorry," I said. I did sound like a robot.

She touched my arm, and her smile partially repaired itself. "Thank you," she mouthed.

I didn't know precisely what I was sorry for—sorry for her loss, sorry for leaving, sorry for mixing her with Amanda Creen in my head, sorry for staring at her hair, all of those things—but it didn't seem to matter. Her smile and that "Thank you" hung with me for hours. All the way out to the crematorium. It was there like a puzzle in the back of my mind as I helped five men—including John Barton—load the coffin onto the rollers to take it into the furnace. It was there while John Barton drove the hearse back home at a slow crawl and spoke reverentially about the process of combustion of human remains. I was listening. Seven hundred degrees Celsius. Half an hour, and the moisture was gone. Another half-hour, and brittle bones remained. I was listening, but something was glowing inside me: a single ember fanned by the memory of Nadia Cooper's smile.

John Barton had work to do in his office. He sent me in for a cup of tea.

Mrs. Barton was on the phone. Skye was slouched on the sofa, Moggy curled on her lap. The television bellowed.

Skye watched me enter the kitchen. Mrs. Barton smiled.

"What are you doing?" Skye asked.

I held up the kettle.

"Who said you could?" she sneered.

I flashed my teeth at her, and the next thing I knew she was there beside me, the cat under one arm.

"You need permission. You can't just walk in and help yourself."

Mrs. Barton excused herself from her conversation and covered the mouthpiece. "Leave him alone," she growled.

"Who gave you permission?" Skye asked again.

"John Barton, your father and the owner of this fine establishment," I said.

Her mouth tightened, trying to hold in her smile of victory. She'd made me speak again.

"He's not the boss of the kitchen; I am."

"Skye!" Mrs. Barton hissed. She flicked her hand, but Skye didn't react.

"You have to ask me for permission."

The cat mewed dismally.

I lowered myself onto a knee. We were face to face, and I bowed my head. "Dear Skye, boss of the kitchen, may I please be allowed to make your father and myself a cup of tea?"

"As long as you make me a hot chocolate."

"It would be my very great pleasure to make you a hot

chocolate," I whispered. "If you would be so kind as to tell me how you like it."

"Milk warmed up in the microwave, three spoons of chocolate, three spoons of sugar, and one marshmallow. White."

"Excuse me for one moment, Mrs. Creen," Mrs. Barton said, and put the phone down. She grabbed her daughter's sleeve and spun her around. "That's enough, Skye. Get out. Watch TV or go to your room. Leave Aaron alone. He has work to do."

The smiles vanished—the wry one on Skye's face and the one glowing in my memory. Mrs. Barton had been talking to a relative of Amanda Creen's, possibly her grieving mother, and I'd been playing games with Skye. Skye dropped the cat and stomped off. She slammed her bedroom door, squealing fiercely something that only the walls could understand.

Mrs. Barton's eyes narrowed at me. "Don't fire her up. Ignore her and concentrate on your work."

I nodded sharply and watched the kettle as it boiled. I splashed my hand filling John Barton's favorite cup, but the scalding barely registered. I didn't make a cup for myself. I didn't make a cup of hot chocolate for Skye either, but I knew I would. One day.

Back in the cool-room, John Barton stood beside the body of Amanda Creen. He was holding her hand.

"This does not look good," he said.

He showed me her fingers. The nails were almost black.

11

NERIDA LONG—THE WEATHERED and crinkled wife of the park manager—was perched on the arm of Mam's chair in the annex. She gripped Mam's hand. Mam looked as though she'd been crying.

"Here he is," Nerida Long said. She stroked Mam's fingers and lowered her hand gently to the armrest. "Home at last!"

"What happened?" I asked. "Is everything okay?"

Nerida Long beckoned me outside. She stood close—too close—and whispered, "Mum's a little confused. She was in Wendy Swain's kitchen. Thought it was her own."

Her voice expressed concern, but her lips suggested glee.

"You might have to keep an eye on her if she's going to be doing this every day. Who's David? That her husband? She was saying he was coming home for dinner. I didn't say nothing. She been to see a doctor? And what were you doing in the ladies' the other day? Hey? Candy says you was in the loo. What were you doing in there? Hey? Don't make me have to kick you out or ring the cops, will you? Hey?"

"Mam had an accident . . ."

"Oh? You don't go in there, though. Under any circumstances, okay? Come and get me if you need to. I'm only too happy to help, but I don't want you going in the ladies'. Hey? Catch my drift?"

She touched my arm and I flinched.

I nodded my understanding and ducked inside.

Mam was watching *Deal or No Deal* as though nothing had happened. At the sight of me, her brow wrinkled.

"About time you got here. Dinner's spoiled again. Where have you been?"

"I've been at work, Mam. Don't worry about dinner; I'll fix it. Who's winning?"

"Hey?"

"Who's winning on your show?"

"Everybody," she said triumphantly.

Mam dried the dishes. She was meticulous and slow as the tide, but she got it done. I was in no hurry. My body ached for sleep, but my head wouldn't switch off. The day kept bubbling around in there without any mercy. I had never meant to annoy Mrs. Barton. Or Nerida Long. I'd touched a dead girl's hair, and it had . . . opened something. I'd said sorry to another girl—possibly the same girl in my jumbled mind—and the opening had torn further. If Mam had another accident, I wouldn't be calling for Nerida Long; I'd be taking her into the men's. Nobody would question that.

There were big signs on the beach warning people never to swim alone. I couldn't read them in the dark, but I would have ignored them anyway. It was partly the danger that made the beach my own. There was the unknown, the dark, the cold, and the emptiness to contend with out there, but those concepts are all relative. Cold compared with what? A dead hand? Dark compared with what? Unblinking eyes? At times the ocean seemed full beside my emptiness. At times it was the one knowable thing in my world.

12

THE AIR IN THE ROOM *is hazy, acrid, and burned. Beneath the ringing in my ears, I hear my own breathing. My heartbeat. The toe moves — a faint twitch — and terror swallows me whole. I run, but movement is beyond me. I scream but make no sound.*

"You all right, mate?"

The voice punched through, and the scream from my nightmare slipped past my lips and into the reality of the day as a kind of yelp. My limbs suddenly started working, and I flailed.

The voice persisted. "It's okay, mate. You're okay. Here, sit up."

I was on the sand. Full daylight seemed some way off. The old man helping me wore running shorts and a fluorescent-yellow singlet. His forehead was glossy with sweat.

"Can you tell me your name, son?" the man asked.

I nodded and rubbed my face.

"Can you say your name?"

"Yes," I croaked. "I'm Aaron Rowe."

"Do you need an ambulance?"

"No, I'm fine."

"Where do you live? Should I call you a taxi?"

"No," I said. I scanned my surroundings. Had I slept all night on the beach? I distinctly remembered curling into bed after my swim. Yes, I still wore pajamas. I took a deep breath, shivered. "I'm staying in the caravan park."

"Here, take my hand," he said. His fingers were hot and smooth. "Let's get you on your feet. The caravan park, you say?"

"Yes."

"Well, that's not far, is it?"

I shook my head.

The cold had made its way deep under my skin again. My teeth chattered. My legs threatened to cramp.

"How'd you end up out here? You a sleepwalker?"

I didn't answer.

"My youngest son was a sleepwalker. Thought we'd lost him at one stage. Turned up in the linen closet. Would have been a laugh, but it was the neighbor's closet."

By the time we got to the pedestrian turnstile, my limbs had unlocked. I thanked the man and apologized.

He held up his hand. "No trouble at all, Aaron. You might want to have a go at tying yourself to your bed. Worked for our Jason."

He waved and jogged back along the beach.

The shower chased the ice from my limbs, but my core was slower to recover. Drug addicts on the beach had knifed people before. It would have been so easy for the man to step around me and pretend I didn't exist. Maybe he saw his son there on the sand? Perhaps the pajamas were a giveaway? In any case, his kindness gave me something bright to ponder, and breakfast tasted better because of it.

Mam whistled on her way to the ladies'. I remembered the tune from my earliest days. It seemed an irreconcilable irony that she could summon that long-forgotten song but still called me David. That the light could fall brightly enough on that part of her mind but leave the can opener in the shadows. I hadn't even considered taking her to the doctor. Or maybe I had but dismissed it just as quickly on account of the complications that might arise. If Mam was having a bad day, she might impress the doctor so much that he'd lock her up. Getting Mam to the other side of town on a weekday was an arduous task, and the doctor didn't work on weekends, did he? Then there was the fact that Mam wasn't physically sick, and trying to convince her she needed treatment risked the very pointy edge of her wrath. And until recently she'd had moments of strangeness in a powerfully lucid world. How the tables had turned. As if a fuse had blown or a bearing seized. Some part of me was still waiting for her to snap out of it.

13

I TIED MY OWN TIE. It took four goes, but I remembered the knot, and the effort now was to get the lengths right before I started looping and tucking. John Barton noticed, tilted his head, hitched the knot this way and that, and then beamed.

"Well done, Aaron. You catch on quickly."

The cool-room stank. It was an evil brew of gas and decay. John Barton made a noise of mild horror, as if he'd remembered he'd left the stove on, then tutted when he found the source of the smell. Amanda Creen's body had changed. Her perfect skin had blotched and discolored; her eyes were sunken and black. The beauty of the day before was gone. Now she was the decomposing corpse of a person who had suffered a violent death. A bruised and wilted rose.

Her toe moved. I could have sworn it. I saw it from the corner of my eye, and my dream flooded in unchecked.

I made a noise like Moggy's and crashed into the trolley on my way out. I ran past the office and into the foyer. I pulled up, panting, in the bright sunshine just outside the front door. John Barton appeared two seconds later.

He grabbed my shoulder. "Aaron? You okay?"

I nodded quickly.

He seemed unconvinced. "Here," he said, and patted the edge of the concrete urn. "Sit for a bit."

I did as I was told and eventually found a rhythm to breathe by. John Barton stared. "What happened?"

"I . . . I . . ."

"Yes? Take your time."

"I . . . It was nothing. Just my imagination running wild."

"What happened?"

"I thought I saw her toe move."

John Barton nodded thoughtfully. He sat on the urn opposite. He pointed toward the cool-room. "That's the other ten percent. The dark side of what we do. It can be a little . . . unhinging. Mess with your head. The suicides, the murders, the babies, and the car crashes. Some of the things we see are truly horrible. There's nothing—"

"It wasn't that." I interrupted.

John Barton blinked.

"I didn't sleep very well last night."

"I hope it's not the work that—"

"No. No, I . . . The work is satisfying. More than that. It's what I want to do."

John Barton exhaled. "If that's the way you feel, then we'll nut it out. We'll do what we need to do until you find your feet. It may take a while."

I nodded, thankful.

He guided the conversation back to practical things. "After an autopsy, bodies tend to decompose very quickly. If we were to open her up, we'd find her guts in a plastic bag. They take a slice from the major organs for pathology and stuff the rest back in no particular order. Short of pickling her in embalming fluid, there's not much we can do to stem the natural breakdown going on."

When I looked up, he was watching me again.

"You okay?" he asked.

I gave him my most convincing nod. Short of pickling my head in embalming fluid, there didn't seem to be much we could do with the natural breakdown going on in there, either.

"Now, I have to go and ring the Creens. Somebody has to try to convince them they *don't* want to see their beautiful daughter one last time."

Before he left, he drove the hearse onto the grassy verge and left me with the hose and bucket of cleaning gear. It was exactly the mindless job I needed. It gave the day some sunshine and purpose. I entertained myself with the notion that I was scrubbing and polishing the shadows from my own mind. The dream couldn't reach me in that sunshine. Mam was fending for herself, and I'd pick up the pieces when I got home if I had to. What I didn't know couldn't hurt me.

"Aaron?"

I didn't recognize the businessman until he removed his hat. It was the man from the beach.

"It *is* you!" he said.

I nodded. My defensive shields were down. This total stranger had seen me at my weakest. He'd also rescued me from my dream.

"Twice in one day," he said, to fill the awkward gap. "How ... extraordinary."

"Yes," I said.

"Your hearse?"

"No, my boss's. John Barton."

"Ah. Good man, John Barton. He's laid to rest quite a few of our nearest and dearest. You're a funeral director?"

"In training."

"How . . . extraordinary."

There were seagulls cawing overhead, but they didn't fill the hole I'd left in the conversation. I took words with my tongue and forced them out. "Thank you."

"What for?"

"Your help this morning."

"It was nothing," he said dismissively.

"No, it was something. It was very kind."

He shrugged.

"I could have been anybody . . . a drug user, violent criminal. Anybody."

He chuckled.

Blood stampeded to my cheeks. I bent to polish the wheel rim.

"In one of my previous lives I was a paramedic," he said quietly. "You develop a capacity to read situations like the body on the beach. And I told you, my son was a sleepwalker, too."

Thinking about it drew me right back to the breathless edge of the dream.

"You're not a paramedic anymore?" I asked, desperate for distraction.

He scoffed. "No. That was thirty years ago. I teach emergency care to nursing students at the university."

"Mam used to work at the university," I said. It was out before I had time to think it through.

"Mam? Dr. Mam Rowe?"

Of course he'd know her.

"Aaron Rowe! Are you related?"

"No." I couldn't keep the sharpness out of my voice. I couldn't keep the syllable from sounding like the lie it was.

The man looked confused.

"She's a family friend," I said. "Known her for years. She taught me how to read and write."

"Seriously?" he said. Then his face softened, and he replaced his hat. "Couldn't think of a better tutor. I bet she taught you a lot more than that."

I nodded, forcing a smile.

"She's one of the brightest people I've ever met," he said. "Do you keep in touch?"

"Oh, I still see her now and again."

"How is she?"

I tossed my rag at the bucket but missed. "She's okay. She's good. Lively as ever."

"That's good to hear. When you see her next, tell her I said hello."

"I will," I said, even though I didn't know his name.

"Better get to work," he said.

"Me, too."

"Ah, the day's too good for working," he grumbled, but he walked up the hill toward the university anyway.

"Thank you," I shouted at his back.

He touched the brim of his hat and waved. "Anytime."

14

I ASSEMBLED A COFFIN FOR Amanda Creen. A white Crenmore Seraphim. I inserted a mattress, but John Barton told me not to bother stapling the silk lining over the plastic. Mercifully, he dressed her while I was working in the storeroom. I held my breath as we lowered her in, and he screwed the lid on tight. The air quality in the cool-room improved instantly.

Except for the sealed box, the cool-room was empty for the first time since I had begun working there. John Barton had me scrub and disinfect the floor, the walls, and the surface of every bench and trolley in the place. Like cleaning the hearse, the work had an easy tempo and tangible results.

John Barton shook his head. "You clean as if you've been doing it for years."

I have, I thought.

"Not just *well,* but as if you have pride in the outcome. That is a rare and admirable trait, and I thank you. How are you with a vacuum cleaner?"

I laughed. It flew from my mouth like a bird, and John Barton smiled.

I vacuumed the office, the chapel, the foyer, and the entry to the public bathrooms. I found a mop and bucket in the storeroom and cleaned the toilets, too. I vacuumed the display room and the viewing room as well. I picked up a JKB Funerals business card from the counter and tucked it in my pocket.

"You're a whirlwind," John Barton said, and I jumped. "A hurricane of clean. Can you handle a lawn mower?"

I dropped my shoulders, which made him smile just a little.

"After lunch, perhaps."

Skye was in front of the bawling TV. She was still in her pajamas—a pair I'd seen on the floor of her bathroom on my first day. She looked my way and wrinkled her nose with displeasure.

Lunch was a huge plate of Mrs. Barton's crustless sandwiches. I picked out the egg ones until I realized John Barton was hunting through the pile for the same thing and I'd taken the last. I offered it to him. He took it and stuffed it into his mouth.

"I have a pair of coveralls that might fit you," he said, his words garbled. "Save your suit from grass stains. They belonged to your predecessor, who wasn't nearly as tall . . . or as handsome . . . as you are, but they'll fit you better than mine would, for certain."

I felt my cheeks grow warm at the flattery.

The coveralls were a perfect fit if I tied the arms around my waist and wore the crotch halfway to my knees. Worn like that, they almost concealed my ankles. I put on earplugs and safety glasses from the cool-room.

The mower in the garage was a newish gas-powered beast

that looked as if it had been cleaned and serviced as regularly as the cars. It started at first pull, and I was hardly surprised. I mowed the verge where I'd washed the hearse. I mowed the front lawn of the residence and—just as I thought I was finished—John Barton shouted that I should mow the backyard as well. It was bigger than it seemed. It stretched beyond the clothesline and around the side of the house near the lounge windows.

I became conscious of someone watching me and discovered Skye frowning from the window. She was behind the curtain, holding the cat, and she brought a finger to her lips.

I pretended I didn't understand.

She shushed through her finger again, and I poked my tongue out at her. Her mouth formed an O, then she poked her tongue out, screwed up her face, and shook it at me.

The next time I looked, she was gone. I took my eyes off the grass for only one second but still managed to hit something. The mower rattled and slapped and eventually died.

I found a skipping rope bound tight around the drive shaft. I popped my earplugs and lifted my green-spotted glasses to the top of my head, then laid the mower on its side. The engine ticked, and I knelt and touched the blades hesitantly.

Footfalls on the freshly mown grass. Skye's bare toes.

"They're not even your coveralls, Robot," she whined.

"Shouldn't you be at school, dear princess?"

She ignored me. "They're Taylor's. You have no right to wear them. Get them off and go and buy your own."

"Taylor doesn't need them anymore," I said.

She sighed and sat.

"You'll get grass on your pajamas," I said.

"So?"

The skipping rope had drawn incredibly tight around the shaft. There was a loose end, but pulling on it with all my strength had no result.

"That's my skipping rope you've destroyed."

"Terribly sorry."

"Taylor gave me that."

"Did he? Then I am doubly terribly sorry."

She scoffed. "Doesn't matter. I never used it anyway." She plucked grass and threw it at my shoes.

"What happened to Taylor?" I asked.

"Dad caught him fondling a dead body," she said flatly.

I almost swallowed my tongue.

"It wasn't even a girl."

I stood up. "I need to . . . I have to get a tool. To cut the rope."

Skye stood up, too. "That's pretty sick, isn't it?"

"Well, I . . ."

She stared at me, her mouth crooked with disappointment.

"Yes," I said. "That is quite sick."

She followed me into the garage and stood beside me as I searched the sparsely populated shadow board for a suitable implement. Pliers. And a sturdy craft knife.

She followed me back to the mower and dropped to her knees on the grass.

"I thought you said you were shy?"

"I am. Sometimes. Most of the time."

"Not with me."

"So it seems."

"Why not with me?"

"I'm not supposed to be talking with you," I whispered.

"Why not?"

"Your mother said . . ."

She sneered. "Who cares what she says?"

"I do. She's my boss."

"I'm your boss," she said.

"Right."

"Pick up that leaf," she ordered.

I handed her a leaf.

"Thank you, slave."

She spun it between two fingers. "Why aren't you shy with me? Is it because I'm a kid?"

"Perhaps."

"Taylor used to give me money. No reason."

I snickered.

"No," she said. "I didn't mean that you should give me money. You can if you want. I just mean that he was generous as well as being sick."

"It wasn't that. Having a conversation with you is like watching television with a monkey when the monkey has the remote. You change channels so fast."

She smiled at that. "I think you're a bit slow, Robot. Batteries flat? Try to keep up."

John Barton appeared from the garage, wiping his hands on a paper towel. The hair stood up on the back of my neck, and I dug at the skipping rope with renewed vigor.

"What's going on here?" he said.

"Robot ran over my favorite skipping rope with the lawn mower," Skye whinged.

"Robot?"

"He sounds like a robot when he talks, don't you, Robot? Say something, come on."

"This does not compute," I said, and John Barton laughed.

"Yes, you're right. He does sound a bit like a robot."

"Do it properly!" she said.

"Leave the poor guy alone," John Barton said. "When you can no longer tolerate this obnoxious child, Aaron, feel free to head home. You've done more than enough for one day. You can fix that next time."

"I'm nearly there." I lied. "Princess Skye isn't bothering me at all."

"See?" his daughter said. "I'm not bothering him *and* I'm a princess. You listening, Father?"

He lobbed the ball of paper towel at her. She ducked, and it bounced off the side of her head. John Barton chortled, then picked it up on his way into the house.

"What's it like living in the caravan park?" Skye asked.

"Some days it's okay. Quiet in the winter. In the summer there are lots of tourists. Young people from Europe, mostly. And retirees in huge vans."

I'm not quite sure what happened then. It seemed as if I'd cracked open the next day's ration of words.

"Actually, there are bits about living at the park that are horrible. Like sitting on a toilet seat warmed by someone else's posterior. Like hearing every detail of my neighbor's domestic disagreements. Like metal music at three o'clock in the morning, not loud enough to disturb the managers on the other side of the park but loud enough to keep me awake. Like stepping over drug paraphernalia on my way to the loo and listening to strangers vomit."

An unsettling stillness came over Skye. Her chin rested on her knees as she hugged her folded legs.

"Sorry. I . . ." I said.

"It must be hard to get any privacy," she said. Her voice had grown soft, contemplative.

I nodded.

"Hearing people vomit makes me feel sick, too."

"I think that's fairly normal," I said.

"You can use my bathroom," she offered.

"That's kind of you, Princess, but your bathroom is a pigsty."

"Ho! Is not."

I looked at her, eyebrows raised.

"Okay," she said. "It's a pigsty. But it's not syringes or spew, is it?"

"True, and I thank you."

She fell silent again.

"What's it like living next to a funeral parlor?" I asked.

She huffed. "It's great. It's all dead people and crying people and flowers and sad music. I'll swap you any day."

"Have you ever seen a dead person?"

"Of course. I see them all the time."

"You're allowed in the mortuary and so forth?"

She nodded.

"How do you feel about death?"

"What? Fine. I'm used to it."

THE DEAD I KNOW

"Has anyone close to you ever died?"

"No. Not really. Not since I was little. When my grandfather died. I don't remember much about that. You?"

"I . . . Is it spooky at night?"

"Has anyone close to you died?"

"I think I'd get spooked at night."

"Have they?"

"Yes."

"Who?"

A long time passed before I answered. Too long.

"Skye?" Mrs. Barton hollered. "Get in here. Now!"

"Who?" she asked again.

"I know about death."

15

WE CRUISED THE AISLES at the supermarket, and it was a cruise. I'd lucked upon a fresh new trolley that hadn't yet developed attitudinal problems. Mam whistled the same tune.

"What's that you're whistling?" I asked.

She answered without hesitation. "It's the opening phrase from Bach's Fugue in D Major. Rosy little tune, isn't it?"

Rosy? Vigorous, perhaps. A little military.

A large soft cube—twenty-four rolls—of toilet paper landed on top of the bags of fruit.

"I think we're okay for toilet paper, Mam."

She shrugged. "It always gets used."

"We don't need it."

"I think you'll find we eventually will."

"No," I said. "Never."

"Hah! How can you say that? Are you renouncing toilets?"

"I *will* use the toilet. We live in a caravan park. The management supplies all the toilet paper we'll ever need. We don't need our own. Not a single roll."

She grinned. "Yes, that's correct. This is recycled paper. They're on sale."

"Not a roll."

She patted the slab.

I slowed and waited until she was out of sight in the next aisle, then propped the toilet paper atop a display of biscuit tins. Around the corner, she'd struck up a conversation with a hoary gent close to her own vintage.

"I agree," the man said. "But what's the alternative?"

"Buy the spices and mix them yourself. There's a whole rack of them here. Aisle six, I believe."

She scurried around my trolley and toward the dairy refrigerator, scanning and touching the shelves as she passed.

The man watched her go and continued his shopping.

He wouldn't know, I thought. He would see a lean older woman, dressed well and groomed—neat, but not ostentatiously wealthy or stylish. The tiny conversation they'd had would reveal no evidence of her frayed edges.

She came back with four bottles of dishwashing liquid.

I thanked her and stashed them back on the shelves in the canned fruit section. Our roles had changed, and I *felt* it.

I knew, from my deepest self to the very skin of my teeth, that I would do whatever I needed to keep her safe from the world. If that harridan Nerida Long had to stick her nose in our affairs, I'd find a way to discreetly break it. If that lowlife Candy from fifty-seven or any of her circus decided Mam was there for the taking, I'd take them out, one by one. Cleanly, without remorse.

◉ ◉ ◉

Two men entered the men's room while I was locked in a cubicle that evening. They spoke quietly, but I could understand every word.

"Mum's fine, but Dad's losing his mind."

"Yeah? What makes you say that?"

"Oh, lots of things. Constantly misplacing his glasses and the car keys, can't remember what day it is . . ."

"Sounds like me!"

They cackled, then went silent. Urine drummed on the stainless steel.

"No, but Dad has always been so sharp. Never missed a trick."

"How old is he again?"

"Fifty-two. Fifty-three in November."

"Bit young to be going senile, isn't he?"

"Didn't know there was an age limit."

"I'm guessing. I don't know much about that stuff."

Their voices trailed into the night, and I was left with all the free toilet paper I needed and a sense that Mam and I might not be alone.

That night, I used my JKB tie to bind my wrist to my bunk in the annex. I lay there for a long time, staring at the distorted green stars through the panel in the ceiling. I figured it would take more than a tie to hold me down, but less than a bunk dangling from my wrist to wake me as I wandered the night.

16

I TRACE THE SHAPE *of a foot beneath the pink sheet and see a leg, the round of a hip. The body is twisted, and the linen is drawn tight across the back. A time-lapse flower of red blooms there. The stain rushes out, threatening to fill the room.*

I hit reality as hard as if I'd fallen from a tree.

I sat up, befuddled but still in my bed. The bed I'd gone to sleep in. One end of the tie was still hot around my wrist, the other draped across my blanket. It had come loose during the night but had obviously been enough to curb my somnambulism. I stared at the tie for a long time, quietly marveling at how simple the solution had been and thanking the anonymous man—Mam's friend the runner—for handing it to me.

The gents' was empty. I was at the mirror shaving when Westy—from van fifty-seven—entered. His face was drawn, probably from lack of sleep more than the early hour. Our eyes met, and he smiled with all the warmth of an autopsy scar.

"Hey, hey! 'Row, row, row your boat,'" he sang. "I 'member you from school!" He slapped my back and laughed bourbon fumes in my face. "Told you I never forget that stuff. 'Member me? Westy? Dale West? Hey, they were prize pajamas you were almost wearing last night, Rowie."

He moved to the urinal and farted as he relieved himself. "Mate, you were out of it. My mum thought you were hot. You'll have to come over this afternoon and stretch out, if you know what I mean. Hey? Fancy a bit of the old Candy on a stick?"

I couldn't move, but I didn't have to.

Westy shook, tucked, and wiped his hand on his jeans before slapping my back again and flashing a stained grin at me in the mirror. "My place is your place, Rowie, okay? Anytime."

He grabbed at his crotch with both hands, adjusted his wares, and lurched toward the door. "Anytime!"

It took a good few minutes for my heart to find its groove again. My breathing was sharp, like that of a wild animal having narrowly escaped a brutal death. I finished my shave in a kind of wide-eyed funk.

The shower drummed on my neck, and I rocked beneath its warmth. Had I really spent part of the night in the company of Westy and his mother? Perhaps the tie had failed? Maybe I'd undone it in my sleep? He had no obvious desire to hurt me, and that had a jot of affirmation about it. He imagined I was stoned or drunk or both. Those states were a daily ambition for the crew in van number fifty-seven, so that somehow made me one of them. Unconscious, I'd been at their level. The thought of stretching out with his mother almost made me dry heave into the steam. Whatever really happened, the loss of that particular memory would never be mourned.

◎ ◎ ◎

The white van quietly burbled in front of the open garage, but nobody answered when I called inside. With my brain still fuzzy, I stood there on the gutter not knowing what to do.

John Barton appeared from the office with his mobile phone to his ear and a grimness about his mien I'd never seen. What upsets you if death is your job? He nodded a greeting and ushered me into his van without a word. He juggled the phone and snapped his seat belt home. With the phone shouldered against his ear, he took off. The tires squeaked, and I gripped my seat as we launched into the traffic. He hustled from lane to lane and out onto the highway, the only clues to the cause of his desperation coming from broken bites of phone conversation.

"Of course. Yes. I guess that's to be expected when you're dealing with an impact of this nature. Thank you, Sergeant. Rest assured we won't be leaving until our job is complete. My pleasure. Goodbye."

His phone hit the dash with a crack.

"This may be one of the few vehicles on the planet where there are actually gloves in the glove box," he said. "I'm going to need a pair, and so are you."

Surgical gloves. He thanked me, snapped them on, and then apologized.

"Start again. Good morning, Aaron. It *is* good to see you."

I nodded and squeezed a quarter-smile.

John Barton looked at me strangely. There was an expectant moment; then he said, "And you reply 'Good morning, John; good to see you, too.'"

"Good morning, John," I echoed. "Good to see you, too."

Uneasy chuckles on both sides of the van.

"You are allowed to stay in the van for this pickup," John said with a sigh. "Motor vehicle collisions are the stuff of nightmares for the emergency services and the funeral directors. Chances are we'll be, quite literally, picking up the pieces."

"I'll be okay," I said, and I knew I would be. I could finally see the line drawn in my head. The animal side of death—the gore and the smell and the decay—could make me feel sick but not really keep me from doing what was required. The parts of my new job that filled me with abject and irrational fear, that twisted me into all kinds of knots, were the raw emotions of those left alive. It was the living who were the great unknown.

A galaxy of red and blue lights. An ambulance, a fire tanker, and several police cars. A truck on the shoulder with a mangled metal appendage on its bumper that was more modern art than motorcycle. John opened his window.

"Morning, Mr. Barton," the policeman said.

"Morning, Grant. Anywhere we can park?"

"Hope you've brought a bucket," he said. He moved a traffic cone and ushered the van through. The small crowd of service personnel parted at the sight of us, and John crawled to the roadside and parked on the grass ten meters from the front of the truck. The oil stains I'd seen from the road weren't oil.

"Okay?" John asked.

"Yes," I said.

The van door alarm chimed, and we were among the police and the firemen. We collected a hard plastic container from the back of the van, like a small, sleek fiberglass casket, and carried it between us over to the truck. We were steered by the police past paramedics tending the bearded figure of the truck driver huddled under a silver blanket. At the back of the truck, basking in a private lake of crimson, was the mangled body of the motorcyclist. Bones protruded from the black jacket, and it took me a few seconds to realize there were bits missing. The jacket sleeve seemed intact, but its contents had been delivered elsewhere by the impact. One leg was considerably shorter than the other.

"Ah," John said. "Probably won't need to check for a pulse." That's when I realized the motorcyclist had mislaid his head.

We lowered the casket on the edge of the pond. It unlatched like a toolbox, and the lid opened with a disinfectant huff.

"Right," John said quietly. "We'll get as much as we can with one lift."

There were no obvious handles—like feet or square shoulders—to hold. John circled the tangled remains and bent beside the intact arm. He looked up at me, reading my face.

"Grab the jacket," he said, and I found some purchase. A heavy lift—a true dead weight—but we couldn't get the whole body off the road. It scraped and grated over the tar, bumped bloody on the rim of the casket, and eventually came to rest on the plastic tray inside. John straightened the limbs and wiped his gloves and the fiberglass with a small dark towel.

"We can't leave until we've completed the jigsaw," he said. "No missing pieces."

So began an hour of sifting through the scrub and grass on both sides of the road. We had police help, but the point of impact was more than a hundred meters down the highway. A boot—with a foot inside—had turned up in the field about seventy meters from the road. Between us, we collected every bit of bloodstained clothing, every dark human scrap, and every shard of bone. Still, one significant piece eluded us. The search area grew wider and more ridiculous until we were combing the swampy field nearly a kilometer from the truck. Every empty drink can and ball of takeaway wrapper gripped at my stomach. Every old shred of tire suddenly became mortal remains.

I walked in a line with two policemen. Their radios barked and fizzed with static. They yelled back and forth, but their words barely made it to my ears. My head rang with the strangeness of the situation and the sense that we might be searching for the rest of the day; and then I found it.

Pressed among the bright green rushes growing in the drain was an arc of shiny black. I could just reach it without getting wet—the dome of the motorcyclist's helmet, with his waxen head inside. I lifted it by the chin strap.

"Ho!" one of the policemen said. "That's what we're looking for. John's boy wins the cigar!"

I carried it like an odd valise to the casket and laid it gently in position. John, puffing from his own searching, nodded his approval. We fitted the lid and carried the container to the van. I became aware, as John closed the door, that although we'd been conducting the same search, the policemen and I had been looking for different things and for different reasons. They were hunting mortal remains to finish a job; I was hunting the still countenance of someone's son, perhaps a brother, maybe even a father, to bring him a final grace. By giving him grace, I found some of my own. The police protected the living, ambulance officers protected the injured, and we protected the dead. All as it should be.

17

JOHN ANSWERED HIS MOBILE as the garage door closed. With one hand, he helped transfer the casket containing the motorcyclist's remains to a gurney and sent me off to the cool-room with it.

I flicked the light switch and opened the door. The tubes strobed, and the darkness between the flashes seemed cosmic. I rolled the gurney inside, and the chill tap danced on my spine. I could smell a hint of Amanda Creen; at least I thought I could—something turning in the back of the refrigerator. I propped the trolley beside her pale coffin and shut the door behind me on the way out.

I had the sudden urge to clean, to scrub and vacuum and polish until everything sparkled—but everything already sparkled with yesterday's effort. I craved some simple and tangible task that might steer my mind away from the questions it wanted answered. *How do we care for the broken man? Undress him? Wash him? Free his head from his helmet?* Left to my own devices, I'd build him a box and screw the lid on tight. A little privacy. Somewhere to get changed into something more . . . elemental.

"Change of plans," John said upon his return. "We're to take our most recent addition to the coroner for postmortem."

I lit up the cool-room again and retrieved the trolley. John steered while I pushed.

"I wonder . . . with all that modern science . . . if they'll be able to ascertain the cause of death?" John began.

I looked at him askance, unable to work out if he was being sincere or . . . A smile bent his lips.

I smiled, too, involuntarily. He knew he'd got me.

"They need to test his blood. Why they can't send someone around I'll never know. I get the feeling they're all too impor-tant for that."

A fifteen-minute drive, a ten-minute wait, and we were rolling the gurney back to the van with the full casket onboard.

"Now, about your driving," John said as he merged into the traffic. "How much experience have you had? Has your . . . someone taken you for a cruise in the parking lot on a Sun-day?"

I shook my head. Mam didn't drive.

"Then that's where we'll start."

He drove us to the golf club. There were a few cars in the lot, but they were bunched around the entrance to the club-rooms. He parked the van away from the other vehicles, and we swapped seats, my fingers shaking as I took the wheel.

"Controls," he said. "Go pedal. Stop pedal. Gearshift. Hand brake. Windscreen wipers. Indicators."

I wondered whether my heartbeat disturbed him; it was certainly a distraction for me. He told me to start the van. With the gearshift firmly in *N* and the hand brake on hard, I revved the engine, as instructed. By lunchtime I'd reverse parked. It was that easy. Apparently, there are people for whom driving seems natural.

"I had to drive the length of the town with one of the local cops onboard in order to get my license," John said. "Just a lap of the main drag." He shook his head. "Somehow, I managed to fail three times."

He poked at me with a single finger. "Not a word of that to anybody, you hear?"

I zipped my lips.

"Not . . . a . . . word."

We had a deal, as long as he didn't mention the fact that my first driving lesson was conducted in a golf-club parking lot with a mangled corpse bumping around in a box in the back.

On the way to the office, John stopped in the loading zone in front of the newsstand, ducked from the car, and returned with a bag that he unceremoniously dumped on my lap.

"Merry Christmas," he said.

Christmas? In May?

It was a guide to the learner-driver test.

"Read it. Cover to cover. Let me know when you want to do the examination." He looked across, his eyebrows raised expectantly. When I didn't get the hint, he cupped his ear.

"Thank you, John. You're very kind," I said.

He beamed.

He parked at the shopping center. I waited in the car while he visited the post office and the bank. He handed me a fold of cash.

"Payday," he said. "More next week if you behave."

I couldn't bear to look at it. I beamed back, stuffed it in my pocket, and thanked him in a whisper.

I studied the guide between eating sandwich fingers, and again in the afternoon while John discussed arrangements with the families of Amanda Creen and the late Eamon Walsh—the motorcyclist. The road rules seemed logical for the most part; the only real challenges were remembering safe distances and the meaning of obscure signs. I carried the book with me everywhere that afternoon—to the storeroom while I made up Eamon Walsh's coffin (another Crenmore Eternity), to the loo, and to the main residence for afternoon tea. I was flicking the pages and testing myself when Skye got home from school.

Without hesitation and without greeting her parents, she flopped beside me on the couch. "What are you reading?"

I showed her the cover and she read aloud.

"Ooh! Can I test you? Taylor let me test him when he was . . ."

I handed her the book. Somehow John Barton's generosity seemed diluted by the knowledge that he'd done this before. This was a well-worn route. Who was I to challenge the natural process of things? Perhaps I should be buying presents for Skye and giving her my pay? Perhaps I should be in the mortuary fondling men? The thought made me shiver.

"Are you okay, Robot?"

I nodded.

"Sorry," she said.

"What for?"

"Talking about Taylor."

"Don't be silly. You can talk about him as much as you like."

She nodded once, unconvinced, and then flipped the book open. "Where are you up to? Which questions should I read?"

"Any. All of them."

She made an O with her lips and clapped her hands.

For half an hour she did her best to trip me up. I was concentrating so hard that I didn't realize we'd attracted a crowd. When I looked up, John and Mrs. Barton were staring from the kitchen.

I stood, reflexively, with the blood charging to my cheeks.

"What?" John asked.

"I . . . perhaps there's something else I should be doing?"

He waved for me to sit. "When you're done with the questions, perhaps you could give Skye a hand with her homework? Only fair, after all."

He was joking, but Skye jumped on the idea and flipped my book on the couch.

"Skye?" Mrs. Barton chided.

John patted her hand, then gave his daughter a grin.

We did surface areas of simple squares in mathematics. We deduced the culprit in a whodunit exercise for science. We shaded the continents on a world map, and I listened to her read from her reader.

"That's enough, Skye. You'll wear him out!" Mrs. Barton said.

"He's fine, aren't you, Robot?"

I felt that Mrs. Barton was talking to me, so I stood.

"We have a little more work to do," John said. "Nearly time we let the boy go home."

Skye groaned.

I thanked her, collected my book, and followed John to the office. He ushered me into a seat, and I had the uneasy feeling a lecture was coming.

He was shaking his head again but smiling at the same time. "You really are a mystery, Aaron Rowe."

"Sorry," I said. It was half question, half apology.

"No, I mean . . ."

He sighed and took a folder from a drawer. "Your school counselor, Andy Robertson, is a close friend. We're from the same church. When we discussed you, he warned me that you could be reticent, moody, and unreachable. That you struggled with every aspect of schoolwork, and no amount of personal intervention changed that."

I bowed my head. It was true, of course. Robertson had seen the worst of me for over a year. He knew more than most.

"He forgot to mention that you're as sharp as a needle, naturally dexterous, and wise beyond your years. Where was that hiding when you were at school?"

I had no answer and nowhere to hide.

"I don't mean to make you uncomfortable, but I do want you to feel you're safe here. That you are always welcome. I've seen enough in a few days to decide that there's a permanent place for you here if you want it, and I hope you do want it because I see the makings of a fine director in you."

He shuffled through the papers in the file and found one he liked the look of. "Employment declaration," he said. "How would you feel about making this arrangement official?"

How did I feel about anything? Scared? Confused? Jammed and broken in so many ways. I sat there, staring, all locked and disoriented. Tears crowded my vision. They welled up on my eyelids, and when they reached critical mass, they boiled over to my cheeks and finally onto my work shirt with a tiny *puk*.

John stood and offered me his box of tissues, but I wiped my face on my jacket sleeve instead.

"I'm sorry," he said. "I didn't realize it would—"

"It's nothing," I said.

18

MAM'S ARMS LAID on the armrests. She leaned forward in her chair, rapt in the show on TV. I kissed her head and looked at the screen.

"What you watching?"

Her reply was a strange whimper.

"Everything okay?"

"Yes, of course. Why wouldn't everything be okay? Idiot."

I straightened. "Idiot? Who's an idiot?"

"Oh, you are. Who else? There's only the two of us here, and it's not me."

"Idiot?"

"Are you making breakfast? It's your turn. I've been waiting for hours."

"It's dinnertime."

She looked outside, her brow furrowed. "I know," she snapped. "I know all this."

I eased past her into the caravan and could hear her mewling over the subdued din of the TV.

I made toast. There were other options, but toast was fast and breakfast-like. I brought Mam's to her on a tray.

"At last!"

"Sorry. Sorry it took a while."

Her hand shook, her face twisted in pain.

"What is it? What's the matter?"

"Nothing!"

Mam upended the tray and stormed inside, growling. She carried her left arm awkwardly, like an injured wing, and I knew it was something serious. She sat on her bed.

I sat beside her. "What is it, Mam? What's happened to your arm?" The sleeve had grown stiff and dark with blood.

"I don't know. It just started hurting."

"Can I have a look?"

"No! Get off. Get off. Get off. Leave me . . . get out!"

I sat there and she cried. I rubbed her back gently until the sobbing eased. It lasted an hour. Maybe more. Together, one centimeter at a time, we drew her sleeve away from the wound and revealed the source of the blood. Something sharp and pale—a splinter of porcelain or hard plastic—had punctured her forearm halfway between her wrist and her elbow. It was still wedged in the skin.

"Nasty. We should get that out," I said.

Mam nodded and sniffed. She turned her head away. I pinched the protruding stub and pulled.

Mam wailed and shoved me clear off the bed.

"I'm sorry, Mam. I'm so sorry. I didn't mean to hurt you. I'm sorry."

She breathed hard, then moaned like a dairy cow—a sound that made me cover my ears. Cover my face.

I couldn't believe I'd been so wrong. It wasn't porcelain or plastic—it was bone. It wasn't sticking *in* her arm; it was sticking *out.*

I listened to her stuttery breathing and tugged at my hair. I couldn't think.

It was over. The fragile bracing of lies and denial that had held our world in balance had broken with Mam's arm. There was no way I could fix it on my own. She needed help.

She needed a doctor, a surgeon perhaps. And in patching her arm, the doctor was bound to notice her mind flapping about, unhinged. My head rang the way it did in the nightmare, but this was real. The ringing drowned out every sane thought. I breathed and swallowed and heard Mam speaking quietly.

"Well, here's another nice mess you've gotten me into," she said, and chuckled.

I remembered the line. I remembered the face—in black and white—from a scratchy old film. Laurel and Hardy. Somewhere inside Mam's jumbled brain, there were still connections that worked. As if she looked at the world through a combination lock, and only when the tumblers were arranged just so could she understand and be understood.

I understood. We had to get to the hospital. I left Mam on her bed and ran to the pay phone near the office. I considered phoning an ambulance, but I knew that would cost money—lots of money. In my panic, I almost phoned John Barton, but Mam was a long way from being dead, and the thought of explaining myself seemed more daunting than the ride to the hospital.

I called a taxi. They said they'd have someone at the caravan park in ten minutes. That gave me nine and a half minutes to convince Mam our expedition was worthwhile, dress her warmly enough, and help her to the front gate. Carry her to the front gate. Drag her kicking and screaming to the front gate.

"How about we go out for dinner?" I suggested.

"Oooh, that sounds like a good idea," Mam replied.

Her agreement caught me off-guard. I'd prepared a whole spiel in the time it took me to run home from the phone.

"Right," I said. "We'll just get your coat on. Very gently. We'll leave that arm tucked in there, shall we?"

"Yes, I think that's best. Don't want it getting dirty. Don't want dirt all over it. Not my best. Not my best. Not my best arm."

I helped her down the step and into the annex. Every footfall made her stop, wince, and hold her breath. In the first minute, we made it to the door. In the second, to the trash can. At that rate we'd get to the front gate by dawn.

"Perhaps I could carry you?"

"What on earth for?"

"I don't know. It's a special evening. I haven't carried you for a while."

"No."

"Probably not a good idea," I said, but bent to lift her anyway.

She obligingly hooked her good elbow behind my neck and stepped into my arms. I had to look twice to see she was off the ground, she was so light. She shut her eyes and breathed through her teeth against the pain. I shuffled fast for the gate.

The driver tooted as I pushed through the pedestrian turn-stile, bumping Mam's hip and setting her off like a car alarm. She thrashed about wildly. I couldn't cover my ears, but I very nearly dropped her trying to do so.

"I'm sorry. It was your hip! You're okay. Here, stand up."

She wouldn't stand, just screamed, paused for breath, and screamed again.

The taxi driver engaged the reverse gear. The wheels crunched on the gravel as he headed for the road.

"Stop! Wait! Please, we have to get to the hospital. She's hurt her arm, that's all. It's her arm!"

The driver paid no heed, just drove back into the night. I sat Mam on the bench in front of the office and stroked her head until the air raid was over and her breath made evanescent puffs of fog.

"Stay here. One minute."

She nodded.

I used the pay phone again. I could see Mam's foot tapping, but her body was behind the wall of the shop. The phone rang twice.

"JKB Funerals. This is John."

Words balked in my throat; my lungs misfired.

"Hello? Anybody there?"

My lips made word shapes, but the logjam in my throat held fast.

"Hello? This is John. How can I help you?"

Help. I was asking for help, that was all. People did it all the time. I'd just forgotten how.

"Aaron? Is that you?"

The deadlock cleared in a rush of words. "Yes, yes . . . hello, John. Hello, Mr. Barton. I . . ."

"Is everything okay?"

"No. I . . ."

"Take a breath, Aaron. Relax. What happened? Are you hurt?"

I did as I was told, and the world seemed three-dimensional again. "No, I'm fine. It's Mam. She's broken her arm. I was trying to get her to the hospital. The taxi wouldn't stop. I . . ."

"Have you rung an ambulance?"

"No. I can't afford . . ."

"Where are you? I'll come and get you."

"I'm . . ."

"Are you at home? Are you at the caravan park?"

Had Skye told him? Did he work it out for himself? Someone must have been driving the girls to basketball when Skye saw me. Strangely, I was comforted by the fact that he knew.

"Yes. We're out front near the office."

"I know the place. Give me five minutes."

"Thank you."

"No trouble at all. See you shortly."

Mam rocked, her injured arm tucked against her chest.

"Won't be long now."

"Damned bus. Never on time."

"No, always late. I ordered us a limousine instead."

"Limousine's never on time, either. They're worse."

Headlights swung into the driveway.

"Not this limousine. I know the driver," I said. "Ready?"

Mam made some unintelligible noises and stood slowly

when I took her elbow. John had parked but left the engine running. He hurried around to open the door.

"Thank you," Mam said.

"Mam, this is John Barton, my boss. John, this is Mam."

"Lovely to meet you, Mam. Thank you for lending me your boy."

"He's not my boy. He's a man. Like a footballer without the football."

"Indeed. A good man."

When Mam was settled in the back seat, John darted to his door. "Hospital?" he whispered.

"Yes, please. The ER."

John sat with us while we waited in the emergency room. I answered the nurse's questions and filled in the forms. Mam became still and regarded the other people waiting with wide-eyed incredulity. When I'd finished the paperwork, I held her good hand.

John glanced at his watch.

"We'll be okay," I said.

He stretched in his chair and grinned. "I'm in no hurry."

His kindness stirred something in me. I sat there squirming inside for a good hour before I could identify it.

Shame.

His generosity merely pointed out my inadequacy. His kindness neatly framed how unprepared I was for life. I *wanted* him to leave.

Mam dozed. I leaned forward in my chair to stretch, and John patted my shoulder blades, once, twice. I looked up, and the concern on his face was another blow.

"She'll be okay," he said.

I nodded. "You don't have to stay."

He looked at his watch again.

"Might be hours before we see someone," I said.

His shoulders dropped.

"Do you have my cell number?"

I showed him the business card I'd been carrying.

"Give me a call when you're ready to head home, and I'll come and get you."

"Yes," I said.

I think he heard my insincerity. "I'm serious. It's no trouble at all."

"I might stay here."

"Of course," he said. "But if you need me, don't think twice. Just call." He squeezed my shoulder and left.

A nurse came for Mam a few minutes later. I woke Mam gently, and she did her dairy-cow moan again at the top of her lungs. The nurse, unfazed, led her by the good arm through double doors to a bed on wheels. I helped her up onto the bed, her moaning now less bovine and more apelike, with brief breaks for theatrical panting and uncontrolled snorting. She took a swing at the nurse. The woman dodged the blow, but it grazed her cheek. The response was immediate—an anesthetist to sedate Mam and a doctor to pronounce the obvious.

"Seems like your mother has sustained a compound fracture in her left arm. Do you have any idea how this happened?"

"No. She's been distraught since I got home. Perhaps a fall?"

"Perhaps," the doctor said, suspicious. "We'll send her down to radiology and make a decision about our next step from the x-ray. Take a seat."

Hours passed. I turned the pages of a dog-eared *Reader's Digest* until my eyes latched on to an article about sleepwalking. Three percent of children sleepwalk, and only half a percent of adults, I read. It happens when an individual is disturbed during slow-wave, or deepest, sleep—a state that's common in children and young adults but diminishes as a person gets older. Sleepwalkers are usually under some sort of stress. They might sit up or walk around. Their eyes are open, and they sometimes talk but they rarely have any memory of their actions. They normally go back to sleep afterward. A German teenager sleepwalked out of a fourth story window, broke an arm and a leg, and kept sleeping. A sleepwalking woman had sex with strangers. One man drove his car. Another stabbed his mother-in-law to death.

I slapped the magazine shut and tossed it on the pile.

Mam snored peacefully, and the knot in my guts pulled tighter and tighter until I had to move.

A nurse in the hall looked up from her work and smiled. "You all right? Ah, you're with Ms. Rowe. There's been a delay down at radiology. Might be another couple of hours until they can see your mum. If you'd like to go home, we can call you as soon as we have the results. Okay?"

I nodded, though I'd left no phone number.

Nobody looked twice as I left the hospital. The night air made my eyes and nose run. At least, that's what I'd have said if anyone stopped me.

19

MY EARS ARE STILL RINGING. *An angle of shoulder leads to a hand hanging clear of the sheet in the shadow beside the bed. The fingernails are painted. It's the same orange, but the dull light has muted it, made it murky brown. I know that hand.*

I erupted awake in the annex attached to van fifty-seven.

I'd slept on a velour couch, covered in a rank blanket and food crumbs. I kicked an empty can across the floor as I slunk for the door, but it didn't slow me down. I didn't slow down until I was in a shower stall with the door locked and the water running, and even then it was only my body that slowed. I shed my shirt and boxer shorts and stomped them on the tiles.

What was wrong with me? Of all the places my faulty brain could take me for a witching-hour stroll, I had chosen that den of turpitude. From all the possible destinations, why would I choose the exact opposite of a sanctuary? I let the water blast onto my face, but the perversity of my subconscious mind ate away at me from within.

"Rowe?" someone bawled. "Are you in here?"

I didn't answer. My throat closed over in terror. I couldn't
have answered if I'd tried.

Doors banged. He was searching through the stalls. Shower
doors clubbed open. Finally, fingers, and then a face, appeared
over the wall.

Westy's malevolent eyes.

He was gone in a flash; then the door to my shower exploded open. He grabbed at my arm.

I batted him away.

He grabbed my wet hair and dragged me out of the shower,
casting me against the wall of basins and mirrors. My bare hip
banged against a sink, shunting it from its moorings. A pipe
split and hissed icy water into the air.

Westy punched me in the face. It looked like such a casual
swing, but instant pain flooded my head from the point of
contact. I slumped to my knees on the cold tiles, and he kicked
my thigh as if making a desperate shot at goal.

My voice suddenly worked—a guttural bark that echoed
off the hard walls. Men began to trickle in through the door,
but each of them froze to assess the situation.

Blood dripped from my face and diluted onto my naked
thigh.

"Where the hell is it?"

"I don't know," I cried.

"Where is it?"

"I don't know what you're talking about."

There was a commotion at the door. The red face of Tony
Long—the park manager—emerged from the bodies.

"What's going on here?" he roared.

Westy made for the exit. A path magically cleared.

One of the residents—a pensioner with faded tattoos and a silver handlebar mustache—moved past the stunned figure of Tony Long and took my arm, helping me to my feet.

"You all right, son? Can you stand?"

I felt my lip, and my hand came away bloody.

"We'll get you in the shower, hey? Wash a bit of the mess off."

He helped me back into the stall with the broken door. It rested closed. I listened to Tony Long cursing as I rinsed the blood off, then dried myself roughly and struggled into my wet clothes.

"Bloody hell," Tony groaned. "Broke a door, too! You boys will pay for this. For all of it. You'll be getting a bloody bill, and if you don't pay it on the day I give it to you, youse will be out on your asses. Get my drift?"

I nodded and left, confident that Westy would have put some distance between himself and the bathroom and any sort of responsibility for the mess. I didn't for a minute think he would head to Mam's van, but there he was. I waited outside the door of the annex as furniture crashed. Cutlery jangled, and a spray of breaking glass made me hold my breath.

"It's not in there!" I howled.

He was at the annex door in a flash, teeth bared. "Then where the hell is it?"

"I don't even know what you're looking for. Whatever it is, wherever it is, it has nothing to do with me."

THE DEAD I KNOW

"You were there last night when I got home. You saw me put it away."

"If I was there last night, I don't remember it. I didn't see you put anything away. Not a thing."

He considered me for the longest time. "You're like a zombie, man. If it turns out you stole my cash, I'll put a bullet in your head. Serious."

I set my jaw and nodded, willing him to leave.

He stopped beside the trash cans, lifted a lid, and then slammed it home.

I had no time to clean. I had no time or desire to eat. I dressed for work and walked to the hospital, wired on adrenaline.

The receptionist did a double take when she saw me.

I asked where Mam was. She looked it up on her computer and sent me off to room 206.

Mam had her eyes closed. Propped on a small tower of pillows, she looked as if she'd fallen asleep watching TV, but the screen was empty, as were the two other beds.

"Mam?" I whispered as I took her good hand. No response. The other arm had been covered in plaster from the wrist to the elbow.

"Hello?" said a nurse. "Ah, Mr. Rowe. Doctor wanted to talk with you earlier, and there was no number to call."

"Is Mam okay?"

"Yes, she's fine. We've had to keep her medicated for the pain, so she'll be sleeping for a few hours this morning. She'll be awake again this afternoon."

I sighed. Felt as if I'd been holding it in for days.

The nurse noticed and smiled. "What happened to your lip? Do you need—"

"Nothing. I slipped in the bathroom. It's fine."

She seemed unconvinced. "Wait here, and I'll go and get the doctor."

"No," I said. "I can't. I have to go . . . to work."

"Is there a number there Doctor can call you on? He wanted to talk with you about your mum's condition."

I handed her the JKB Funerals card.

"Oh," she said. "I see. Are you a funeral director?"

"In training."

She nodded reflectively, reading the small print on the card. "I'll give this to Doctor, and he'll probably call you before he leaves later this morning."

Mam made a noise. A little throaty sigh of contentment.

The nurse patted my hand. "She'll be okay. We'll look after her."

"Thank you," I said. "When she wakes . . ."

"Yes?"

"When she wakes, let her know I'll be back after work to pick her up."

"Doctor may want to keep her in a while longer."

"I'll be back this afternoon; tell her that."

"Of course."

John raised his eyebrows at me by way of greeting. He stared at my lip, waiting for an explanation.

"Slipped. In the bathroom."

"Ah," he said dramatically. "How is Mam?"

"Resting. They've put her arm in a cast. She's still at the hospital. They're taking good care of her."

It wasn't until the words passed my lips that I realized the gravity of that truth—they *were* taking care of her. Even if they noticed a foible or two, they could blame them on the shock of breaking her arm or the medication. The reassuring thing was that someone would be there to stop the beetroot from burning.

"That's good to hear," John said. "I . . ." He seemed suddenly pensive.

"Thank you," I said to deflect his thoughts. "For last night. I don't know how we would have gotten to the hospital otherwise."

"Probably walked, knowing you."

I smiled but couldn't help feeling that the statement was loaded.

"I had a pickup from the hospital in the wee hours. I popped in to see Mam. The nurse said you'd left."

"Had to clear my head," I said.

"Did it work?"

"Not really."

John smiled, touching my sleeve. "You don't have to do it alone."

"Thanks," I said, a little too swiftly. The full stop hung in the air for a long time.

His pickup was an elderly gentleman named Karl Stevens.

If I had been asked to guess at his cause of death, I would have said skin cancer—his head carried scars and small craters where parts had been removed. I fitted out a Crenmore Imperial with its chrome handles and ornate finials. John washed the body.

"That box is a work of art," he said when we were done.

I buffed it with the soft, open-weave cloth reserved for that purpose. It seemed absurd that the coffin would at best be buried, at worst burned.

"Almost six thousand dollars," he said, and I coughed.

He rubbed a spot with his sleeve. "Not the most expensive coffin in our range, but it's up there. Each to his own. My golden rule when choosing a coffin with a family is to provide them with the one they want to buy, not the one I want to sell."

Clothes arrived for Karl Stevens in the late morning. My guts rumbled as we dressed him in an old paint-spattered Hawaiian shirt, faded jeans with holes in the knees, and rubber flip flops that had conformed to the shape of his soles with wear. I could see the pale V on his tanned feet where the flip flops had sat. The people left behind knew him well enough to honor his personality before honoring tradition, or perhaps they were fulfilling his final wishes. Either way, the body of Karl Stevens spoke of a life lived. In my mind, he was an arty beach bum. Casual in life and casual in death.

"I think we'd better go and eat something before your stomach leaps out and has a nip at me!" John said.

"Sorry," I said, and patted my belly. It had been a day since I'd eaten. The protests were justified.

I'd expected a plate of sandwiches, but I got roast beef, as though Mrs. Barton had somehow sensed the ravenous beast inside me.

"Good lord, what happened to your face?" Mrs. Barton asked.

"Slipped in the bathroom."

"That's what they all say," she said wryly.

"It's the truth." I lied. Well, it was only a *little* lie—more an omission of facts than fabrication.

She paused midway through serving peas and regarded me intently. I'd protested too much.

I tried to smooth it over with a manufactured smile, and she continued spilling the peas onto the plates, the table, the floor.

"Look out," John said. "Now you've made her pea on the floor."

Mrs. Barton dropped the spoon in the pot and slapped him on the arm.

"Ow," I said.

"Did you hear that, dearest?" John said. "You slapped me so hard, you hurt young Aaron."

"Bah," she said. "He's made of tougher stuff than that."

I had to wonder.

The doubt stayed with me right through the meal. It hovered at the back of my mind and spat out images from the nightmare. From the morning. How tough was I, exactly? I couldn't really call what happened with Westy a fight. That implied there had been two parties actively involved. I had done nothing—nothing to deserve it and nothing to provoke it, short of being unconscious and drawn to the wrong place at the wrong time. Why was I drawn *there,* of all places? I had done nothing to defend myself, either.

All those fiery thoughts I'd had about protecting Mam had amounted to nothing. She'd hurt herself, and I'd thrown my hands in the air, content to pass the responsibility of her care to someone else.

The phone rang. I'd been in a stupor, and the ringing cut through it like a two-handed blade.

"It's for you," Mrs. Barton said, puzzled.

I took the phone, my hand shaking. "Hello?"

"Mr. Rowe?"

"Yes."

"It's Doctor Chandra here." His voice was sonorous, accented. "I've been looking after your mother, Mam Rowe, and I wondered if we might have a little chat about her well-being."

"Of course."

"Her arm will be fine. We undertook some reconstructive surgery very early this morning to repair the fragmented bone in her forearm, and the operation went well. She will probably be in plaster for a couple of months, but we're expecting her to make a full recovery."

"That is . . . that's great news. Thank you, Doctor. I —"

"A more pressing concern has been Mrs. Rowe's state of mind. She seems disoriented and confused."

"Probably just the accident. Medication. She sometimes seems confused even when she isn't," I said. I sounded insane.

"She has also exhibited signs of being agitated. I wonder if her well-being has been assessed recently? By Mental Health, perhaps?"

"No," I said. It was a flat and sharp response, and it frayed the edges of the conversation for several seconds.

"I see," Dr. Chandra eventually said. "Maybe it would be a good idea to have her assessed while she's here? Mental Health physicians regularly visit the hospital for psych evaluations and triage. It would be no trouble at all for them to make a bedside call."

"No," I said again. I could hear the fear in my voice. "That won't be necessary. I'll take her and have her assessed when she's able."

Another long pause.

"Of course, that's an alternative," Dr. Chandra said. "I'll write a referral."

"When can Mam come home?"

"I'd like to keep her in for one more night to make sure there are no complications; after that she'll be free to go."

"I can keep an eye on her."

"Are you a doctor, Mr. Rowe?"

"No. But—"

"I think Mrs. Rowe would benefit from the professional care given at the hospital. If you're willing to take the responsibility, I can get the release forms ready for you to sign."

I could still see the bone protruding from her forearm, and the thought of it made me unsteady. I knew she would be better off at the hospital, but something clouded my vision. I wanted her home for my sake. Keeping an eye on Mam distracted me from my nightmares, gave me purpose. The weight of domestic tasks filled the blank spots at the end of my day. Sometimes I shrank from my own company. Face it; sometimes I shrank from my own shadow.

"No," I said. "Your care has been . . . just what the doctor ordered. Thank you."

He blew a nasal laugh into the mouthpiece. "Happy to be of service."

Mrs. Barton spoke before I'd hung up the phone. "Perhaps you'd like to stay for dinner? It'll just be soup, but you're welcome to share with us."

John caught my eye. I could feel him reading my face.

"Leave the lad alone, Delia," he said. "He's got enough to worry about at the moment—"

"Thank you, Mrs. Barton," I said, interrupting. "That would be great."

The service for Amanda Creen left me sapped. It was so solemn and quiet, with huge silent gaps where I could hear my own heartbeat again. The bereaved spilled out the door and into the hallway, leaving standing room only amid a colored lake of floral tributes.

The celebrant turned out to be her uncle. He choked twice—they were the times I almost had to leave—but then he breathed, straightened, and spoke some more. His courage kept me at my post. When it came time to press the button and start the committal, John gave me the nod, and my shaky fingers did the deed. Tears hung on my lids and crystallized my vision as I whispered my own goodbye to Amanda Creen.

When the last of the mourners had left and we'd loaded

the coffin and the flowers into the hearse for the trip to the crematorium, I slumped into the passenger's seat and sighed.

John flashed me a smile. "You did well, Aaron. Told you it would get easier, didn't I?"

I nodded.

"Yes, John," he sang. "You were right. It *is* getting easier."

"Yes, John," I echoed, using his silly tone. Then my natural voice struck through again. "Somehow seeing the celebrant cry made that one bearable."

"True," John said without a trace of a smirk. "He was very good. Damned sight better than Charles Walton."

The fat man in purple and green. Compared with Amanda Creen's uncle, he seemed shallow and insincere, as though the reason for the gathering was as much about listening to him as it was showing respect for the dead. That didn't explain why I'd been able to stand and watch Amanda Creen's uncle struggle with his pain. Why I'd become teary but had not broken down. The speculation poked me in some dark, bruised places, and I gave up trying to understand before I did some real damage. Knocked off a scab. Punched open an old wound.

20

I TIDIED THE CHAPEL WHILE John made calls from his office. Quiet footsteps on the carpet shook me from my cleaning daze.

Skye smiled.

I grinned back at her effortlessly.

"Can you help me with my homework again?"

She seemed out of place, standing there in the light from the stained glass. A little too bright for the room. A little too vital for the languid postfuneral air.

"Of course," I said. "I'm almost done here. Better check with your father."

"Don't worry about him," she blurted.

"But I will," I said. "That's my way."

"The robot code of conduct?"

"Precisely."

"I'll check," she said in a monotone. She turned on her heel and scuffed mechanically out of the room.

I shook my head and listened.

John murmured a greeting, to which there was no reply.

"Robot's coming to help me with my homework," she said, and I winced.

"Try again, sweetness," John said.

She sighed. "Father, dear, could I please use your robot to do my homework?"

"Of course, darling. Please don't wear him out too much. He's staying for dinner."

"Really?"

I'd forgotten. My breath snagged, and I thought about Mam for the first time in hours. I couldn't stay for dinner; who would look after her?

I remembered the hospital, but the panic didn't ease. I had a sense that she wouldn't be coming home, that they'd sink their claws in and put her in a box for broken people. The sense was so strong and alarming that I ran from the chapel and straight into Skye. She hit the floor and bounced.

"I'm sorry, Skye," I hissed. "I can't stay. I . . . I . . ." I left her there and sprinted to the office.

John stood, my own dread mirrored in his face. "What is it? What happened?"

"I . . . It's Mam. I have to go."

"Calm down, Aaron. She's okay. She's at the hospital."

"You don't understand. I have to —"

"She's okay," he said again.

"I can't explain. I have to —"

"Stop!" John bellowed.

I stopped, just for a moment. Just long enough for my eyes to focus — on John Barton, red-faced and stern.

"Mam is okay. She couldn't be in safer hands. Safer there than at home, wouldn't you agree?"

"But . . ."

"Wouldn't you agree?"

"Yes."

"Now take a big breath."

I took a breath, but it wasn't big.

"Good. Now hold it. That's it. Now exhale."

"There are things I haven't explained. She—"

He raised a finger. "Another deep breath. Fill your lungs. All the way. More. Hold it."

I felt lightheaded. My heart thumped a death-metal groove into my temples.

"Hold it."

Somehow the breathing and the holding short-circuited my fright. When I exhaled the next time, I felt my shoulders relaxing and rational thought returning.

"Well done. As soon as I'm finished here . . . one phone call . . . we'll get into the Merc and pay Mam a visit. Okay?"

"Can I come, too?" Skye asked. She stood behind me in the doorway, apparently unscathed.

"If it's all right with Aaron," John said.

I nodded, then turned and put the nod into words. "Of course, Skye. Sorry I bowled you over."

She shrugged. "Anytime."

John laughed and shook his head. "Give me five minutes."

I opened the garage door and sat on the curb. Skye sat beside me.

"Was that a panic attack?" she asked. "It was, wasn't it? My mum has them. Usually about stupid things like forgetting to top up the water in the vase or leaving the cat inside when she goes shopping. What was yours about? Your mum or your mam or whatever you call her?"

"Mam. Just Mam."

"Why Mam?"

"That's her name."

"I call my mum Delia sometimes. Usually when she calls me Skye Rose Barton. Two seconds before she whacks me with whatever she has in her hand. Does Mam belt you? Not now, but when you were little?"

I shook my head. Not when I was little. She'd never even raised her voice at me. Never needed to. It wasn't that I was an angel; anger never seemed to find purchase in Mam.

"Did she hit you in the lip? Why would you have a panic attack about her? She's at the hospital, isn't she? It's supposed to be the mum worrying about the kid, not the other way around. I couldn't think of a safer—"

"It's not as simple as that."

"Why not? She allergic to hospitals? Scared she might fall in love with a doctor and leave you?"

"You ask so many questions."

She shrugged. "I'm a kid. It's my job."

"And you have a theory about everything."

"Inquiring mind. Is that a crime?"

"Yes."

She was silent for a brief moment, and I thought I'd found her Pause button.

"Why isn't it simple?" she said. "Is it the drugs? Is she an addict like you? Oh, she's your supplier, and you'll go crazy if she's locked up in hospital. You'll get withdrawals and start seeing pink elephants and have imaginary creatures crawling under your skin."

"You watch way too much television."

"Maybe," she said. "But it doesn't stop me wanting to know."

She looked at me, through me, her eyes like those of a predator with prey in sight.

"I have this dream," I said. "Recurrent. I've had it since I was a kid. Nightmare, really. Lately I have it every time I go to sleep, and every morning I . . ."

The sound of jingling keys in the garage.

"Right, you two," John said. "Let's go."

"You can sit in the front," I said to Skye.

She sighed. "I'm not allowed."

"You can sit in the back."

"Thank you."

"Not a word," I whispered.

"About what?" she hissed. "You didn't tell me anything. You have nightmares. Whoo!"

21

MAM CALLED ME AARON. She clunked my head with her cast as she hugged me from her bed and laughed an apology.

I introduced the Bartons, and she said she remembered John from somewhere. I told her about the mercy dash he'd done.

"That's right!" she sang. "Of course."

She didn't remember, but the act was flawless.

"How are you?" John asked.

"Oh, you know, up and down. Down and up."

John laughed kindly.

"You've come to take me home, then?" Mam asked.

"I think the doctor wants to keep you in one more night, just to make sure everything is okay," I said.

"Does he, now?" Mam said, suddenly indignant. "We'll see about that!" She swung her legs to the side of the bed.

I grabbed her knees. "You wait here; I'll go and discuss it with him."

"You're a good boy, David. I'll wait here, then."

"David?" Skye chuckled. "Who's David?"

"I am," I said. "Aaron David Rowe."

Skye looked at her father. "You start calling me Rose, and I'll put salt in your sugar bowl."

"Can't have that," John said. "Better watch my tongue."

"Rose is a pretty name," Mam said. She reached for Skye's hand.

Skye let her have it but didn't step any closer to the bed.

A nurse paged Dr. Chandra. Apparently he hadn't gone home after all, or perhaps he was back in already. He arrived in a coat-flapping jog two minutes later, shook my hand limply, and led me by the elbow into a small room with a sink and a fridge.

"Cup of tea?"

I shook my head, looking him in the eyes. He straightened his tie.

I brushed mine flat, instinctively.

"Your mother is in good physical health. I have no reason to doubt she will regain the use of her arm completely."

There was an unspoken "but" at the end of the sentence, and I held his gaze.

"I think there may be some impairment to her cognitive functioning. Do you understand—"

"Yes."

"All I'm asking is that you approve some noninvasive testing of her perception and memory. It's a courtesy, really. Mrs. Rowe has already expressed her consent."

"Mam's already said yes?"

"That's correct."

"But she doesn't know . . ."

It was too late. Of course she'd say yes. She'd say yes to toilet paper if they offered, too. Protesting on the grounds that she didn't know what she was agreeing to would be admitting the truth—she really didn't know what she was agreeing to.

Steam hissed in my veins. I wasn't ready to let it go. I wasn't ready for them to be poking and prodding Mam. I needed more time. Mam needed more time. She could wake up tomorrow, and everything would be the way it used to be.

Dr. Chandra must have felt the steam. He took half a step back.

"No," I said through my teeth. "No tests. I told you, I'll get her assessed myself when she's back on her feet."

Both his hands came up. "Okay. Fine. I can only offer my recommendations."

"Then she's free to go?"

"I would like to keep her in for one more night. Without injected pain medication, she will be uncomfortable. She'll sleep better here."

"But no tests."

"No tests."

I wondered whether I could get some injected pain drugs for myself. Anything to make sleeping easier. Anything to stop the film running night after night in my head. I considered taking Skye up on her offer of period-pain medication, and a smile tugged on my lips.

Dr. Chandra leaned in. "It is possible for you to sleep here," he whispered. "To put your mind at ease. Not policy, but possible in certain special situations."

"No," I said. It came out like a hammer blow. "Thank you, but I have things to attend to."

He inclined his head politely.

"Thank you," I said again, the steam now safely contained.

Skye and John were a little wide-eyed when I returned. John took his car keys from his pocket.

"One more night of pampering for you, Mam," I said.

She slapped her thigh and grinned. "Where did you put the TV remote, Aaron?"

I was about to protest until I spotted it on her bedside table. I pointed instead, kissed her gray curls, and left her to poke buttons.

Skye held her father's hand as we threaded our way through the maze of corridors. I walked beside her, and when I paused to take stock of the signs overhead, she grabbed my fingers with her free hand and tugged me into motion.

"This way, Robot," she said. "Car park."

"Right," I said. "I knew that. I was just computing the possibilities."

She chuckled but didn't let go.

Mrs. Barton's soup was more of a stew, and for some reason the smell reminded me of candle wax. I had to force the last ten spoonfuls down out of respect for the feelings of the chef, but I got there in the end. Even managed to politely refuse a second helping.

I cleared the plates, and Mrs. Barton berated me for attempting to wash the dishes in her own house.

"Don't do the dishes if you don't have to," Skye said. "That's just stupid. Besides, you have to help me with my homework, remember?"

"You're incredible," John said with a laugh.

I sat with Skye, and she opened her book but didn't look at the page. She looked at me, eyes brimming with curiosity.

"How come she's so old?" she whispered.

"Homework," I chided.

"She's older than my grandma. She's old enough to be *your* grandma."

I tapped the page and she picked up a pencil.

"What is your dream about?"

"Nothing," I snarled. "Concentrate."

"I am concentrating. What's it about?"

"Skye, stop it."

"What's it about?"

"I'm not sharing my dreams with you."

"What's it about?"

I faked a yawn. "Goodness, is that the right time?"

She grabbed my sleeve. "No, sorry. Don't go."

I stared at her fingers, and she smoothed and patted my shirt. She read math questions aloud in her best robot voice, pecked at the problems, and eventually finished the page.

"We're done?" I asked.

"No! There's English. I need help with . . . I need help with a story. Tell me one."

"You make one up."

"Okay, you give me ideas, and I'll make one up."

"I'm supposed to be helping, not doing it for you."

She tapped the pencil on her chin and stared at the ceiling.

"There was this boy, right?" she began. "He was born in another country. Maybe Canada. Yes, Canada. But his mum and dad didn't want him anymore, so they sent him to live with this old witch in another country. She gave him drugs and turned him into a robot, then the boy . . ."

"Enough!" I cried. I stood up, knocking Skye's books to the floor.

She shrank, her eyes wide. "Sorry."

"Enough."

John appeared at my side. "How about I run you home, Aaron? It's been a big week. Nice lazy weekend will do you wonders."

I collected my jacket as he ushered me to the door. I didn't say goodbye.

22

SORRY," JOHN SAID as he pulled up in front of the caravan park. "Skye can be a handful at times."

I'd made some sort of recovery from the shock of having a cartoon of my life story plucked from my head. "It wasn't her; it was me."

I thanked him for the lift and closed the door as quietly as I could.

I'd given her snippets of my world, and she'd done no more than paste them together. I'd underestimated her powers of perception. I wouldn't be doing that again.

I found the sliding door of the annex open. I remembered the morning's fracas and thought I might have left it that way, but Mam's chair had been overturned and my mattress was on the floor. I didn't remember that.

Movement in the van caught my eye and stalled my pulse. Curtain in the breeze.

Westy had definitely been back. The contents of every cupboard, every drawer, every shelf, in the van had been methodically emptied onto the floor. Dried herbs mixed with broken eggshell on a bundle of Mam's undershirts. The fridge door had been propped open by an upturned milk carton. A charred mess on the stove turned out to be a pair of my boxers.

I cleaned. I started at one end and scooped and washed and scrubbed and wiped until the bins were full and the entire place sparkled. No hint of burned beetroot or underwear, just the fake pine smell of surface spray.

I walked to the beach. I threw myself—fully clothed, sans shoes—into the crushing cold of the ocean. I panted at the surface and ducked under the feeble waves. My lip stung, but I convinced myself that it was a pain of healing, that—like the cold needling the rest of my body—it was a rite of purification.

Exhausted, I dragged myself back to the van. I slept in Mam's bed the way I'd done when I was little. I locked the annex and the door of the van and hid the keys in the grill. I tied one end of my JKB tie to my wrist and the other to the bedside lamp, which was screwed to the wall. I breathed and turned and waited for sleep as if waiting for a punch.

23

THE PINK SHEET DOESN'T *rise or fall. It almost covers the head. A curl of dark hair lies flat on the pillow. I see parted lips, and they are full and womanly, slack with sleep or death. A nostril is haloed in blood.*

I woke as if I'd come up from beneath the earth, puffing and shaking and gulping for air. It was still dark. I'd slept three, perhaps four, hours. My tie had cut the blood flow to my fingers, and my hand had turned a deathly blue. I tore at the knot, managed to tear the light fitting from the wall, and made my wrist bleed with the chicken scissors while cutting myself free.

My tie was ruined. The keys were gone.

The door of the van opened when I tried it. The sliding door was off its runner. The keys were in the lock.

I scurried to the showers and punched the tiled wall of the shower, trying to restore feeling to my fat fingers and banish the desire to kill something. Anything. I punched until my knuckles bled and the exasperation flowed from my eyes as mute, salty tears.

Any trap my conscious mind set, my subconscious could avoid. I don't know why that surprised me — we were the same

person. Weren't we? "Zombie," Westy had said. A zombie
aware enough to untie and retie knots, search out keys, uproot
doors, and have less than a blink of memory of the proceedings.

I stopped punching the wall when the shower chilled in
response to a toilet being flushed. I turned the hot tap off
completely and wore the full icy blast of spray on my upturned
face.

I shivered as I dried myself, my limbs leaden and stunned
by the cold. I felt tired to the marrow, the lack of sleep and the
relentless imagery of my dream gradually swallowing the last
of my defenses. Amanda Creen's moving toe, my panic attack
in the chapel, and my reaction to Skye's clairvoyant storytelling
were products of my sleep-starved and addled brain. The less I
slept, the less I *could* sleep and the more fragile my mental state
became.

A lazy weekend, John had prescribed. The thought of staying still long enough for the dark thoughts to sink their teeth
in kept me moving. I washed and dried my work clothes and
ironed everything that had a seam. When the sun was properly
up, I jogged along the foreshore all the way to the hospital.
Right through to room 206.

Tucked-in sheets wrapped the bed where Mam had been
the night before. Like an actor in a comic play, I looked under the bed and in the cupboard before I realized what I was
doing.

"Mam?"

Movement in the corridor.

"Mam?"

A nurse entered. "Mr. Rowe?"

"Yes."

She squared her shoulders, resting a hand on my elbow. "Your mum's been taken up to the Herriot Wing. If you'd like to come with me, I'll show you the way."

She dragged me by the elbow, more than practical urgency in her stride.

"What's the Herriot Wing? Why has she been moved?"

"Herriot is the critical care unit. I'll let Doctor explain the full details of why she was moved."

"Critical care? What happened? She had a broken arm!"

"She's okay, Mr. Rowe. Honestly. They transferred her up there to keep a better eye on her. That's all."

I stopped in my tracks. It broke the nurse's grip.

"No," I growled. "Tell me the truth."

She flushed. "See for yourself," she said, beckoning.

It became a monumental effort for me to move, one step at a time, through the fire doors marked HERRIOT WING. The nurse led me on to a dimly lit room where Mam slept—a picture of tranquility. I breathed again.

"She's fine," the nurse said, her hand on my arm. "Doctor will be with you shortly. Have a seat if you like."

She left and I chose to stand. I took Mam's hand, limp and warm, and held it to my cheek. She didn't stir, and I knew she'd been medicated. Even at her most deranged, she slept like a bird, woken by the slightest sound or movement. She was usually awake when I got up, as if her consciousness preceded my own. In my childhood, when nightmares woke me, she'd be speaking words of comfort before I fully realized I'd been dreaming. At Easter and Christmas, with the expectation of chocolate eggs or gifts like caffeine in my veins, she'd be wishing me good morning before I'd rubbed the sleep from my eyes. This fake torpor was the closest I'd seen her to death.

"Mr. Rowe?"

I dropped her hand. "Yes?"

It was a different male doctor, taller and younger, with a pair of livid scratches on his right cheek. He shook my fingers and said his name—a swatch of syllables I couldn't keep hold of.

"Mrs. Rowe is sleeping. We have given her a sedative."

I nodded.

"She woke during the night," he said. He touched the wounds on his cheek. "She was confused and distressed. We transferred her to critical care so that she could be watched on a more regular basis."

"Can I take her home now?"

"I would advise against that at the moment. In her current state—"

"She's confused and distressed because she's here," I said.

"Probably true," the doctor said. "We had to reset her arm after her outburst."

"I could bring her back in if—"

"That would be an ideal situation once her arm has had a chance to stabilize. Perhaps a couple of weeks."

I felt the injustice in my guts. It swam around and pulled the muscles of my face. He didn't realize what he was saying. He was saying, "You'll have to balance your tottery world without this strut. You'll have to face up to things without this protective blanket, live life naked."

I wasn't ready for that. At that moment I felt I never would be. I could see my fears were irrational and pathetic. I could see it would change little about my day-to-day life; in fact, it would make certain aspects of my life easier if Mam was safe in hospital, but she was my lifeline—my conduit through which the world made a strange sort of sense. Where would I hide?

"If you need somebody to talk to, I can . . ."

I wiped the expression off my face and tucked it back in its box. I reined in my breathing. "I'm fine," I said.

It was what he wanted to hear, even if it wasn't the truth. He offered a curt nod and left the room.

I kissed Mam's forehead and fled.

24

I WANT TO MOVE, *but I no longer want to run. I want to pull the sheet away. I want to see the face. I want to know the texture of the fabric, feel its bloody weight, and be steeped in its terror. I must move, or this moment will eat me alive. I close my eyes, and I know that someone is watching me. I feel it on the back of my neck. I turn my head.*

I leaped awake as if my heart had been jump-started with a defibrillator. A noise made it through my lips, more squirrel than human. A green shadow recoiled from in front of me and retreated to the door of the annex before I'd rubbed my eyes awake. Somebody *had* been watching me.

Saturday afternoon. I'd fallen asleep in Mam's armchair studying my guide to the learner's permit even though I told myself I wouldn't, shouldn't, couldn't slumber. I'd woken exactly where I'd fallen asleep for the first time in a long while, the book still on my lap. The television spoke too fast and too loudly. The silhouette of a child hung in the doorway.

Skye Barton. She smiled, flicked a wave. "Sorry. Didn't mean to scare you."

I killed the TV. "No, you didn't. I just . . . I was dreaming."

She stepped forward. "Was it the same dream?"

I nodded before I could check myself, rubbed my temples.

"Tell me. What's it about?"

"How did you find me?"

She shrugged. "I was at Steevie's place. Just kept looking. Steevie went home."

I stood.

She backed outside into the light.

"What are you doing here?" I asked.

"I don't know. I got bored. Dad was supposed to come and get me an hour ago, but he phoned to say he had to do a pickup."

"So you thought you'd come and watch me while I slept? Is that it?"

Her cheeks colored. "I wanted to say sorry."

"For what?"

"For last night."

"Apology accepted," I said. "I should be saying sorry to you. I reacted badly."

She took a step closer. "So, what is the dream about?"

"Is that really any of your business?"

"No. But that's not going to stop me from asking, is it? I'm a kid. I'm supposed to be blunt."

I gave a joyless snort.

She smiled in victory.

I sat on the step into the van, waving her to Mam's seat. She wriggled into place, then stared at me, expectant.

It's difficult to say why I spoke to her. It was probably a mix of things—her age, her curiosity, her persistence, her honesty, her familiarity with death. I found myself speaking with ease, painting that one scene again and again until every detail lay bare. Maybe it was Skye; maybe it was me. Maybe I was going mad. Maybe I was already mad, and talking to Skye was one way of admitting it to myself.

"That sounds real. It isn't just a dream, is it?" she said. "Look! I've got goose bumps. How much of it is real? Is the blood real? Who is she?"

"Enough," I hissed. "It's a dream. I should have known."

"What? Should have known what? That I wouldn't stop? What do you think I am? I'm a—"

"Kid. Yes, I know."

"I was going to say girl. It's in our nature, you know. Talk, talk, talk. Ask a thousand questions. Comm-uni-cation. I thought robots were programmed to communicate?"

"Too much communication," I rattled. "Must ... shut ... down."

Way off in the distance, a voice bellowed.

Skye swore, covered her mouth, and apologized. "It's my dad," she whispered. "See you!"

Her shoulder hit the sliding door as she ran through. She apologized again but didn't break her stride.

It was after eleven when I sneaked to the empty shower block and brushed my teeth. The lights seemed friendlier than I remembered. I stopped brushing to listen—footfalls on the path outside. It was too late to hide.

I stooped over the sink. Westy entered my peripheral vision and stopped. It wasn't an abrupt stop—his limbs seemed heavy and loose.

"Rowie, Rowie, Rowie," he said, tutted, and shook his head.

I didn't look up or acknowledge his presence.

He moved swiftly, with fabricated poise. He grabbed the hair at the back of my neck and butted my head into the mirror. The glass cracked obligingly, but he didn't let go. I tried to shake free. He turned my head and slapped the side of my face with his free hand. My ear rang as it had in my dream. He slapped me again, and toothpaste spit sprayed us both. He shoved me off in disgust. I caught hold of a sink and remained upright in the corner against the shower stalls.

Westy unzipped his fly and hauled his penis out. He stretched it and flapped it from side to side, took aim, and relieved himself on the floor, on my leg, my hip, my stomach. I'd turned to stone. Cold, hard stone. He rolled up onto his toes, and his stream reached as high as my chest. I closed my eyes until the flow diminished to a series of squirts accompanied by little grunts.

He spat, hitting my shoulder, and then left.

I stood there, dripping, his vapor hot in my nose. *Pea on the floor.*

Two steps into a shower stall and a battering of ice needles. It took ages for the water to warm up and even longer for the smell to leave. Someone had stashed a bar of soap on top of the wall between the stalls, and I shed my clothes and scrubbed until the only smell rising in the steam was bogus lavender. I padded back to the van barefoot and naked, unseen and unheard, and dumped my wet things in the rubbish.

I couldn't live like that anymore. I lay on Mam's bed and

caught bites of party noise from van fifty-seven that set my heart on a wild gallop. What had I done to unleash the mindless wrath of Westy? I hadn't touched his cash. Without the distractions of work and caring for Mam, I had nowhere to hide. If it wasn't for the total numb exhaustion, I would have run. Wherever. Forever.

25

A SINGLE RED EYE *is hovering in the shadowed doorway. It shakes, as if bitten by rage. I have stared at it for a lifetime, but in the dream it is scarcely a second before it suddenly blinks and floats to the height of a man. The eye is the glowing tip of a cigarette. The smoker inhales, and the glow sketches the figure. I know him. It is the man she calls David.*

Dawn on the laundry bench. I'd fashioned a pillow from forgotten clothing and woken with a crowd of thoughts protesting in my head. *David?* The dream was no longer a single scene. It had morphed and taken on new dimensions, and the fear I felt had multiplied, too. It now had a face—one I didn't want to remember but somehow did. I knew that if I let my thoughts rest there, the face would crack and release a buzzing swarm of memory.

I showered and walked along the shore to the café strip. The day shimmered, the air still and bright. I felt strangely rested, as though the shift in my dream denoted that I'd surrendered to my fate, whatever that might turn out to be.

I bought a cooked breakfast and ate it on an al fresco table beside a woman with a newspaper, a boyish dog, and a cigarette. She sent me a smile, and I lobbed one straight back.

"Magnificent morning," she murmured, her words thickly accented.

"True," I said.

At the sound of my voice, her dog stepped as close as his lead would allow and pressed his nose to my thigh. He watched my face with his hazel eyes, searching. I scratched his head and whispered a greeting.

"Wally, get down," she said—definitely French. "The poor guy doesn't want you slobbering all over him." She reached under the table for Wally's lead.

"He's fine. The attention is always welcome," I said.

She smiled again and tugged on his collar anyway. "Yes, he's not exactly the perfect gentleman, but he is the friend of the *entire* world."

I held that thought for a mere slice of a second—*friend of the entire world*—and my eyes flooded. Not with television tears, but silent, hot things that dripped faster than I could wipe, that made my nose run and fuzzed my vision.

"Are you okay?" the woman asked. Her chair scraped and she handed me a serviette.

I thanked her, nodding. I squeezed my nose on the paper towel, mopped at my face, and sat there. Meet the incredible crying boy. See him *feel* something before your very eyes.

The woman went back to her paper, polite enough to not make a fuss and brave enough to sit there as I melted. Perhaps tears were commonplace in her life? The crying lasted less than a minute, but it left me feeling as though my lungs were bigger than they were before.

The woman bade me farewell with a smile.

"Thank you," I said.

She nodded and tugged Wally's lead. Her high heels clicked loudly on the pavement; the dog's claws clicked softly.

Mam's hospital bed had a blue seat belt. It had been drawn across the blankets over her hips. It was loose enough that she could slip out if she wanted to but tight enough to remind her to stay put. Her good arm wore a tight circular bruise I hadn't noticed the day before. Her face wore a grin for me.

"Here he is!" she sang. She'd blanked on my name completely; I could see it behind her eyes. "Give me a hug."

I did as I was told, and there was a kindness about her touch that took me back to childhood. Just for a breath.

"What have you done?" I asked, gently stroking the purple mark on her arm.

"Oh, it's nothing. Not even a scratch."

"No, it's a bruise."

"Nothing."

A nurse entered, one I'd not met.

"Here she is," Mam said. "Come and give me a hug."

The nurse, to her credit, took the embrace sincerely but with a smile. "Can't get enough of them," she said. "Do you need the toilet at all, Mrs. Rowe?"

"Fine at the moment, thank you."

The nurse tugged on the belt, tightening and then loosening it as if to remind Mam of its presence. She made a quick check of the machine beside the bed and left silently.

"I knew you'd come," Mam said, and patted my hand.

"Of course. Can't let you have all the fun."

"You remind me of my son," Mam said.

"Astonishing coincidence," I said mockingly.

"True," she said. "Your eyes, particularly."

"And what is your son's name?"

She looked at me, her face suddenly empty. "You know."

"Do I?"

She slapped my hand, and it reminded me of the petulant Skye. "Well," she said. "If you don't know, I'm not about to tell you."

With that fragment of conversation, I knew the scales had tipped. Mam had gone and probably wouldn't find her way back. She'd done her work. She'd schooled me in life the way an institution never could. She'd made me think long and hard about everything and anything, answered every question I'd ever asked and many that I hadn't. She'd fed me, washed me, and clothed me until I could do it for myself. Until I could do it for her. She'd grown old, and now she was growing young again, all innocence and hugs. It seemed to have happened so fast, but if I stopped to think about it, I knew there had been years of incremental decline, faithfully denied by us both until *paf,* like a blown globe, she'd finally let go. Until that moment when I'd let go, too.

What is life without a memory? Is it death? Sometimes memory was death—slow and painful, eating away at your insides, reeking of decay. Losing your memory would save you from that, wipe your slate clean. But the good would be swept aside with the bad. All the fine things to build a life on would be lost, leaving you just one thing—that moment. No dreams and no history. The ultimate expression of living in the now. There was nothing sweet or philosophical about holding Mam's hand, however. She knew she was going to prison. One without walls or bars, where she'd be bound to forget and bound to ask the same questions over and over until she forgot how to ask. Forgot how to speak. Forgot how to eat. Or live.

Out of nowhere, Mam began to cry. Her face crumpled, and she bowed her head and rocked.

"What is it, Mam? Are you okay?"

"It's nothing," she sobbed. "Not a scratch."

My arm over her shoulder, I wept for the second time that day. Wept for the future. Wept for the past. Wept for the nothing in between.

All the objects, sights, sounds, and smells that once coalesced to make home broke apart and re-formed while I was away that Sunday. I could not settle. Being lost within the borders of the familiar was the scariest thing I'd ever experienced. What was once a cocoon now felt like a cracked shell.

The racket spilling from van fifty-seven fueled my restlessness. The music was loud, but the voices punching through were louder and as sharp as razor blades. Something bad was going down, worse than usual. Maybe I was hearing them clearly for the first time.

Getting ready for bed, I wondered if I could second-guess

my subconscious by bedding down someplace irrational to be-gin with—beneath the bushes along the beach, under the stairs at the lookout, behind the Goodwill bins in the supermarket parking lot. If my dream-self arose in an unfamiliar bolthole, perhaps I'd head for the caravan. Yes, and perhaps I'd head for van fifty-seven. I imagined what it would look like to a casual observer seeing a strange, lean figure in pajamas stepping over the fence and bedding down in the coastal heath with the windblown rubbish. Vagabond of unsound mind, which didn't seem too far from reality. I understood how a homeless person might evolve. It wasn't necessarily some grand calamity that displaced you to the streets; it might happen gradually over a lifetime, with each step along the way making sense. It made perfect sense to me, and I would have slept out that night if the air hadn't been so cold and damp. Ah, my kingdom for a bed with a seat belt and a nurse to lock me in.

26

HIS CHEEKS ARE WET. *His lips move, but I can't hear his voice. My ears are still ringing. He limps awkwardly from the shadows, leaning heavily on a crutch. He is naked. Claw marks score his chest and thigh, some weeping red. His teeth flash as he speaks. He takes a long drag on his cigarette and shakes his head. His crutch is a shotgun.*

So cold.

"Sir? You okay? Sir? Can you hear me?"

Somebody shook my shoulder, and I leaped to my feet, sucking air.

"It's okay. We're here to help."

The hand was back on my shoulder again, comforting now, warmth seeping through to my frozen skin. I rubbed my eyes frantically.

Policewomen—two. I'd woken on the pavement in front of the café where I'd eaten breakfast the morning before. I couldn't feel my bare toes, but in the feeble light I could see they were covered in sand. I'd walked the whole way—more than a kilometer, and certainly a personal best.

"Can you tell me your name, sir?" the woman with her hand on my shoulder asked.

"Rowe. Aaron Rowe."

"Have you been drinking, Mr. Rowe?"

"No. Sleepwalking."

They looked at each other.

A violent shiver rolled down my spine.

"Here," the other woman said, handing me her jacket. "Just put it over your shoulders."

"Thank you."

"Where have you come from, Mr. Rowe? Where's home?"

"The caravan park."

The woman who'd given me her jacket laughed. "Are you serious?" Constable Nadine Price, her nametag said.

"Can we give you a lift home?" the other—Constable Kim Something, with too many letters—asked.

"Thank you," I said.

They swapped the jacket for a soft gray blanket and helped me into the back of the police van. I shivered all the way home and thanked them as they let me out at the pedestrian gate.

I handed Constable Nadine Price the blanket, shaking.

"Will you be all right?"

I nodded. "Shower."

"Good idea. Might want to make an appointment with your doctor about the sleepwalking. Hate to see you mown down by a truck."

I summoned a smile and left.

The best thing about the weekend turned out to be going back to work on Monday. In one tempestuous week, the funeral parlor had become my sanctuary. The smell of air-freshener flowers had become linked in my mind to the cool stillness of death, and death was my new best friend—someone I'd only just met but felt I'd known forever.

John was on the phone in the office. He greeted me with a grin and a salute. I bowed and headed for the mortuary. If Skye had been right about the pickup, there'd be a new body to prepare.

Two new bodies, in fact. Both elderly, both female, both wearing pajamas. The kindest way to go. Even if they'd been ill and suffering for months or years, death in bed seemed the gentlest surprise. It wasn't hard to imagine them surrounded by their families as they did the last of their breathing. Said their goodbyes. Kissed cheeks. No luggage to check in. *Leave your body with us,* I thought. *We'll look after that.*

I had a sudden longing. It was as clear as daylight, and the longer John spent on the phone, the stronger it became. I wanted to clean. Something. Anything, really. I checked the public areas and found them spotless, but the urgency turned to action, and I cleaned the toilets anyway. I was hanging the mop up when John emerged, whistling, from his office.

"Self-starter," he said. "That's what I like to see. Morning, Aaron."

"John."

"Good weekend, I trust?"

I shrugged. "Happy to be here."

"Where's your tie?"

I plucked at my collar. "It was . . . damaged. Bit of a long story."

"Damaged or ruined?"

"Ruined."

"Ah, I see," he said.

He left the air empty. I had no inclination to fill it.

"I have another. *One* other," he eventually said.

The room grew still again, and I found the words he needed to hear right on the tip of my tongue.

"Sorry, John. It won't happen again."

His brow bunched, ever so briefly. "No matter. Come."

I followed him through the building.

"We found some coveralls for you at the weekend. Mrs. Barton figured out your size from suit measurements she remembered off the top of her head. Let's see how clever she is."

A sound stopped me in my tracks between the garage and the house. John kept walking.

There it was again, a small squeak. Insect or rodent. I followed it across the yard to the nest of potted plants and found the cat on its side, damp with dew, panting. I moved pots and tentatively stroked its head.

"John?" I called. I'd never used his name like that, and the panic was audible, even to me.

He was there in a flash, eyes big.

"Oh no," he said gently. "There you are, sweetheart. Are you okay? Moggy?" He picked her up, her body spilling limply over his hands.

He groaned. "Moggy? Ah, you poor thing. You've had it, haven't you, darling?"

There were tears in his eyes. His mouth buckled and

straightened. He forced it open, as if to call his wife, but no sound came out.

I jogged to the door. "Mrs. Barton?"

"Yes, dear?"

"We found Moggy. It doesn't look good."

She hurried to her husband, hand to mouth. She stroked the cat, and Moggy's skin quivered. She'd stopped panting, stopped breathing altogether, it seemed.

"Is she dead?" Mrs. Barton asked.

John gently laid the cat on the grass beneath the clothesline. "Yes, I think so."

"Poor thing," Mrs. Barton said, and walked back inside.

I watched her go, unable to believe she'd just walked away.

John was still for a long time, sniffing quietly and staring at the cat.

"Deal with death every day of my life . . . in one way or another. You can never tell when it's going to bring you undone."

He pinched his nose. "Skye will be devastated."

I had to wonder whether he knew his daughter as well as he thought. Her nonchalance about death seemed as natural as her school uniform.

"Would you be so kind?" John said. "There's a shovel in the corner of the garage."

"Of course," I said. "Did you have a place in mind?"

"Behind the potted plants there. In the garden bed. Just a hole. I think Skye might like to pay her last respects in person. I'll fetch your coveralls."

A smallish wooden box rested on the bench beside the stand

of long-handled tools, the kind a special bottle of port might be sold in. It contained a collection of little shed things—assorted washers, screws, plant tags, and string—and would make a fine coffin for a small cat.

John saw it in my hand and laughed out loud. "Perfect. What did I tell you? You're a natural!"

He took the box, emptied it on the bench, and blew the dust out.

"A clever craftsman could line that with silk," he said. He handed it back. "Might even find a small pillow to fit."

"Are you sure you'd . . ."

He dismissed me with a flick of his hand. "Go to town. Not often do we have a death in the family, thank God."

My coveralls were a perfect fit. I helped John dress the old ladies in the cool-room and spent the rest of the morning preparing a coffin for Moggy. I lined the box with silk, cut a pillow in half—at John's insistence—and stapled it to the thin timber. Moggy had gone stiff by the time the box was ready for her, and I had to close my eyes as I bent her legs to fit. Ten minutes of shuffling and twisting, and I finally settled on a restful pose for her—face-down, slightly on her side, with her legs tucked underneath. When the bereaved arrived, we'd be ready.

The florist delivered a load of wreaths for the funeral of Karl Stevens. A dainty posy had been hidden among the masses of blooms. It had nothing on the card. I showed it to John.

"For the Mog," he explained.

Eighty or so people crammed in the chapel for Karl Stevens that afternoon. Six people delivered a eulogy—two sons, a daughter, a brother, a close friend, and Karl Stevens's wife.

There was a lot of laughter amid the tears. The dead man had been well loved, kindhearted, and generous. The picture they painted of a beach bum wasn't that far removed from the one I'd imagined, and I wondered how I'd be remembered.

I wouldn't be remembered at all. There'd be no family to remember me, no friends, no neighbors to speak of. I'd pass as a footnote of humanity, a poorly attached addendum to be left in the bottom of the box. I knew that John would dress me up and give me a sendoff—I wouldn't be left on the street. As I pressed the button to send Karl Stevens on his way, I felt hungry for a place in the world. Even if only one other soul on the planet felt my passing as something more significant than a raindrop on a gray day, I'd die content. Even if that one soul was an ill-tempered child . . .

I laid Moggy's posy on the dark soil beside the makeshift coffin.

"What are you doing now, Robot?"

Skye had startled me, and it must have shown.

She giggled, but the giggle hit a wall when she realized who was in the box. Her mouth opened and closed but formed no words. The color left her cheeks. She jettisoned her schoolbag, and it toppled a potted plant.

"Moggy?"

She squatted beside the coffin and stared. She reached out but had second thoughts and hugged her knees instead.

"Moggyyyy?"

Tears dropped to the earth, and she rocked, ever so slightly. It was hardly a movement at all, but it felt as though she was going to scream.

"It was very peaceful," I said. "I found her just here, behind the potted plants. As if she'd gone to sleep."

She stood abruptly but didn't wipe her eyes. She turned and wrapped her arms around my waist, buried her face in my suit jacket, and wailed.

I staggered—off balance in more ways than one—then stood firm and tried to stroke her head. Her braids were stiff and opposed to stroking, so I rubbed between her shoulder blades and felt her squirming with the pain. Felt as useless as I'd ever felt.

Her father had been right—Skye was devastated. She held tight, howled and sniffed, blubbered and shuddered forever. She had been wrong about death—she wasn't used to it at all. She'd never really felt it. Other people's dead were like pictures. Moggy—feeble old Moggy—was the real deal. Did I really know death?

To truly know death, you'd have to have loved.

In time, John emerged from the garage. He patted my shoulder and whispered his thanks. He crouched beside Skye and stroked the side of her face. When the feeling got through, she let go of me and latched on to her father's neck. He lifted her off the ground with a groan and shushed her, swaying her gently from side to side.

"Better summon Mrs. Barton," he said.

I did as I was told.

Mrs. Barton made no sound, but tears drained from her face like ice melt.

"Poor old Moggy," John said. "She was as old as you, wasn't she, Skye?"

Skye's head uncurled like a turtle's from her father's neck. She looked at the coffin and nodded.

"She was a good cat," Mrs. Barton said through her tears.

A doleful silence followed. I stood with my hands clasped in front of me and waited. John caught my eye and gave me a nod, but there was no button to press. I stepped forward and closed the lid of the box.

"Can I do it?" Skye asked. She wriggled until her dad released her, then took the coffin and lowered it neatly into the hole. She collected a handful of dirt and scattered it over the wood. I did the same. John and Mrs. Barton took their turns, and then the three of them went inside the house while I filled the hole.

Skye came back red eyed with a fistful of rose petals she'd plucked from the front garden. She waited until I'd smoothed the last of the soil before arranging them just so, then turned to me. "Needs a cross or something."

"Let's see what we can find."

We unearthed a cut garden stake, a nail, some string. Skye wrote Moggy's name neatly on the stake with black marker. I tapped it in place with the hammer.

"Looks stupid," Skye said, and tore it out. She hurled it over the fence.

She levered a flat stone from the garden edge, scrawled on it with the marker, and sat it at the head of the grave. Much more dignified. Perhaps there was a gene for graveside expertise?

27

ALL THE GOODWILL garnered during the day was swept aside when I got home. The sliding door had been forced; the contents of the van and the annex had been upended again. A sickening smell fouled the air. The television was gone; Mam's bed had been stripped and dusted with self-rising flour. The stench came from a loose coil of human excrement, served up at the kitchen table on a plate.

I ran from the van and coughed up the remains of my crustless sandwiches beside the trash cans. Hands on knees, I heaved and breathed until the sound of laughter nearby made me freeze. Westy watched from the half cover of the camp kitchen. When he realized I'd seen him, he swore and ran. My revulsion turned instantly to fury, and I sprinted after him.

He slipped past vans, hurtled pine logs between campsites, and toppled bins and chairs to impede my passage, but succeeded only in slowing himself down. He was still laughing. It powered the rage inside me. He skittered for the front gates, but I caught him by the collar before he got there and rode him to the footpath—literally rode him. Felt the concrete beneath us skinning him. Heard the involuntary grunt as the air left his lungs. Wondered why I'd never done it before.

I had never felt like this before. Never *felt* before. Not in this way. My swing was in full motion, and I knew I could go higher and harder. When Westy moved, it was to cover his head. I tore his shirt dragging him upright, slammed him into the steel Coke sign attached to the wall of the park office. He yelped.

"I have nothing of yours," I screamed, shoving him again, pinning his head against the sign.

"Okay, all right. It was a laugh," he bawled. "Nothing. Calm down."

The office door slammed.

"I'm not laughing."

"Right."

"I'm *not laughing.*"

Tony Long grabbed my wrist in his beefy hand and pulled me off Westy. He tried a cop-show maneuver—twisting my arm up my back—but I flicked and ripped my hand free. He skipped off a safe distance.

"Calm down, Aaron," he said, flashing his palms.

"I'd like to register a complaint."

"Oh? Would you really?" he said mockingly.

"With you or with the police. Your choice."

He laughed. "With the police? This must be serious."

A couple of kids from the houses opposite the park watched from the roadside.

"Come and have a look at the van," I said. I walked. Tony Long followed.

"It was a joke," Westy moaned. "You take everything so seriously."

"Shut up, Dale," Tony Long said. "I've had enough of your crap."

The plate had vanished. Mam's chair was upright, and the bedclothes had been pulled up over the flour. Someone else had been in there in the few minutes since I'd left.

"Can you smell that?" I asked.

"What? I can't smell a thing. Well, nothing I wouldn't expect to smell in here."

I tore back the covers to reveal the mess. The flour had been shaken onto the white linoleum floor where it was all but invisible.

Tony Long sniffed. "What exactly am I looking at?"

"Flour. There, on the floor."

"And that's the complaint?"

"Westy broke into my home. He turned the place upsidedown."

"I thought it always looked like this. Cleaner than Dale's van."

"He stole my television."

"Really?" He sounded unconvinced.

"Yes, really. Look around you. Can you see a television anywhere?"

"That's serious," he said, barely restraining a smile.

My hands became fists.

"You need to calm down, Aaron. If what you say is true and Dale has been in here without your permission, then that's a serious offense. If it happens again, I'd suggest you tell Nerida or me. Right? Under no circumstances should you take matters into your own hands. Catch my drift?"

My teeth clenched of their own accord.

"Do . . . you . . . understand . . . me?"

"Yes," I spat out.

"Where's Mam?" he asked matter-of-factly. "Haven't seen her around for a while."

"Visiting relatives," I said.

"I'll be having a word to her when she gets back. Catch my drift?"

"Yes," I said again, and Tony Long left.

"Oy, Aaron," he shouted from just outside the door. "This your TV?"

It had magically appeared beside the trash can. Placed ever so delicately in my puddle of vomit.

"Yes," I said once more.

"I think you'd better get your facts straight before you start flinging around accusations."

He sounded like a soap opera, but at least I knew where I stood. Dale West would always get the benefit of the doubt, and in a showdown—my word against his—he would win before I'd even spoken.

The plate of poo had been dumped in the trash can. I found it while emptying the vacuum cleaner bag. It seemed Westy had an accomplice to pull his asinine pranks with. There was only one thing I could think of more damnable than Dale West, and that was Dale West squared.

The sun had gone by the time I'd finished cleaning. I could have eaten, but the thought of making more mess and then cleaning up again seemed to be too much effort, and I was too keyed up for there to be any hope of sleep. I changed into a black tracksuit and walked to the hospital.

Mam was no longer in intensive care. A nurse informed me that she'd been taken to Finch Ward and that visiting hours were finished.

I hung my head. It wasn't an affectation; I did feel the walk had been for nothing. The nurse patted my shoulder.

"Let's see what we can do," she whispered. She beckoned me along the corridor, turning this way and that until I was totally lost, eventually arriving at the doors of Finch Ward. She punched a code into an electronic lock, and I felt my stomach tighten. What kind of hospital ward needs locks on the doors?

The first thing I noticed was the noise. The moaning and crying. The ward sounded like a medieval dungeon. The air wasn't quite right either; in the battle between human and chemical smells, humans were winning.

Mam was propped up on pillows, watching television.

"Mrs. Rowe?" the nurse said. "You have a visitor."

She didn't flinch, just stared at the screen.

The nurse smiled as if to say good luck as she left.

At Mam's bedside, I bent to kiss her curls.

She turned on me with her teeth bared and slapped my face with enough force to make both my ears ring.

"What did you do that for?" she howled. "What did you do that for?"

She slapped me again, but I'd covered my head, and the blow cuffed my forearm.

I backed away, and she was straight out of bed and after me, scratching and kicking.

"No. Card. My. Ass," she bawled, punctuating with her fist and stockinged feet against my body.

The attack stopped as abruptly as it had begun, and I uncovered my face to see Mam struggling with two nurses. A scream—animal and spit flecked—burst from her lips as she thrashed against their grip. One of the nurses called a name, and a female doctor arrived and administered an injection in Mam's behind. Mam lost her footing almost instantly, and she flailed in the nurses' arms for the longest minute before they lifted her back on to the bed.

"Are you okay?" the doctor asked.

I nodded.

She rested a hand on my shoulder and surveyed my exposed skin. "Gail, could you tend to these scratches, please."

"Of course, Doctor," one of the nurses said. She took me by the elbow and led me to the nurses' station, where she dabbed something cold on my face. It stung but not enough to rouse a reaction from me. I was numb again.

"Dementia patients can be unpredictable," the nurse said. "Hard to read them at first, but once you get used to their individual quirks, it does get easier."

Dementia. She'd laid the diagnosis out plainly. I'd spent so long denying Mam's behavior and hoping she'd snap out of it that having it acknowledged by somebody else, having the lid taken off the secret that was never really a secret, filled me with relief.

"She'll sleep until tomorrow now," the nurse said. "You all right to get home?"

"Of course," I said, but I had my doubts. The caravan seemed light years away. Heavy-limbed sleep was calling, but it never called in the soft voices of pillows and clouds; it cackled and beckoned with a bony finger.

28

H E'S SHOUTING BUT *it's no use; the ringing in my ears has made me deaf. I feel his wet sputter and the heat of his breath on my cheeks. His black eyes, pinched and cruel, are the hell where my every fear is spawned. He grabs my hair and hauls me across the room.*

The hair pulling woke me, dragging me from the dream. I jerked free, and a hank was torn from my scalp.

Predawn. My surroundings were underexposed and heavy with shadow, but I knew where I was—the cigarette-butt-strewn vestibule of the lookout by the beach.

David was there somewhere; I knew it.

A clap of bird wings made me panic and run, down the lookout stairs—three at a time—onto the sand and to the water's edge. It was a full minute before I could sensibly draw the line between sleep and wakefulness. Clearly, the more sleep-starved and crazy I became, the more fragile the line between the two worlds grew. There was no David—I'd slept on a bench, and my hair had been caught in the seat. My subconscious had painted the nightmare to match my circumstances, not the other way around.

Light rain fell. I hugged myself as I walked and felt it—cool and undeniably real—on my neck. I was still wearing the runners and tracksuit I'd been wearing at the hospital, and to the joggers braving the foreshore track I would have looked like one of them, out to work up a morning sweat. I would have been sweating when I made it home, too, if I hadn't been so cold to begin with.

The van was the way I'd left it. I ate a token breakfast and showered. The scratch on my cheek didn't look as angry. My eyes were bloodshot, and dark circles had formed in the pale skin around them. I could make my hair neat and my tie straight, but I could do little about the state of my face.

John looked twice.

"Morning, Aaron," he said. "Everything okay?"

I forced some extra chirp into my voice. "Yes. Fine. Why?"

He shrugged. "Wrong end of the day to be looking as tired as you do. How's Mam?"

"Stable," I said. I wanted to tell him more. I had the fleeting desire to tell him a lot more, but old habits and the fear of revealing too much made the words congeal in my throat.

"Good," he eventually said.

The welcome breeze of industry swept us up—three coffins to build, a pickup from a private residence in Singer Street, crustless sandwiches and a loud television, flowers delivered and arranged in the chapel, the newcomer to wash and dress in the afternoon. Driving lesson in the golf-club car park.

Every little action, every practical thought, every aspect of the work, recharged my batteries. By the end of my driving lesson, I was in control of the car, in control of my emotions, in control of this one slice of my life.

"Have you been studying your book?" John asked.

"It makes sense," I said. "It's easy to learn."

"We'll book you in for your test tomorrow."

My heart stopped. One beat. Two beats. I'd missed three beats before normal transmission was restored. "Okay."

John sent me inside for tea while he phoned and booked the test.

Skye was tucked up against the armrest of the couch. I smiled at her. She didn't respond. I put the kettle on, but Mrs. Barton shooed me out of the kitchen.

"Go and sit. I'll make the tea," she grumbled.

I sat next to Skye and watched the commercials.

"How you feeling?" I said to the television.

"Fine," Skye breathed. "Except my cat died. You?"

"Okay," I said.

"Your eyes are all black. You've been taking drugs again, haven't you?"

I smiled.

"Steevie says it's easy to spot the druggies on the street because they all look like they're wearing black makeup, but they're not. It's just their skin rotting from the inside out."

"I see," I said.

The ads finished, and a hypercolored cartoon screamed into action.

"How's Mam?" Skye asked.

The monkey had the remote again.

"She's . . . okay. They've put her in Finch Ward. There's a lock on the door."

"Is she crazy?"

"I don't know. Are you crazy?"

"No. Are you?"

I took too long to reply. I should have said *No!* with great conviction, but the truth was hanging there. "I . . . I don't know. Some days I think I'm going around the bend."

Skye twisted her knees to face me. "The nightmare?"

"Everything."

"Like what?"

"Like sleepwalking. Like having the van broken into. Like—"

"You sleepwalk?"

I nodded. The kettle whistled and I jumped to my feet.

"Where do you go?" Skye asked.

I held my finger to my lips and nodded once at her mother.

"Where do you go?" she whispered.

"All over town. Upstairs and downstairs in my nightgown."

"Serious?"

I smiled. It was an automatic defense mechanism. Like a moth with owl eyes on its wings or a lizard with a frill. *Don't get too close, kids; if this creature gets alarmed, he* smiles *uncontrollably.*

It worked. Skye suddenly lost interest. She bit her nail and watched the cartoon.

I took two cups from Mrs. Barton and left, cursing under my breath. I put a cup on John's desk.

"Four thirty?" he mouthed. I nodded.

One day, I thought, *when somebody reaches out the way Skye did, I'll have the guts to take her hand and my world will be a different place. I know it.*

29

H E RIPS THE BLOODIED *pink sheet off the body on the bed. The woman is naked. Her guts are hanging out. He presses my head down so I am nose to nose with the face on the pillow. Her eyes shift, focus, roll, and focus again. She mouths my name. She is my mother.*

I was on my back in the dark. I fought for consciousness the way a drowning man fights for air, thrashing with every muscle. Streaks of red, blue, and white light. I was awake; my arms and feet were pinned by strong hands. I bucked, and they shifted but didn't yield. I screamed in rage against the grip.

"Steady," a voice said. "It's okay. We're here to help. Can you hear me? Take a breath."

I blinked, and a small crowd of unfamiliar faces appeared above me. In fright, I screamed and thrashed some more, but the grips grew uniformly tighter as I did.

"Can you hear me?" the voice asked again.

I felt grass beneath my head. It smelled cool and bruised. How long had I been down here, unconscious? I took a breath and exhaled, commanding my limbs to relax.

"I can hear you," I said.

"Hey? What was that?"

"I hear you," I said, louder.

"What's your name, son? Can you tell me your name?"

"Aaron. Aaron Rowe. I live at the caravan park. Can you get off me now?"

The pressure eased, but the people holding on to me didn't let go. They helped me sit up. The man in front of me wore blue surgical gloves. Paramedic. He touched my brow, my cheek. The glove dragged on my stubbly jawline.

"Where am I?" I asked.

"You're safe," the paramedic said. "Do you feel any pain?"

I shook my head.

"We're going to move you over to the ambulance, Aaron. That be okay?"

I didn't answer, but they lifted me anyway and pressed me onto a crisp-sheeted gurney. They covered me with a blanket, and I realized I was cold. Chilled to the core, again. I shivered.

"What do you remember about last night, Aaron?"

They weren't all paramedics; the one who'd asked the question was a policeman.

I took another breath and collected my wits. Wherever I'd been during the dark hours, whatever I'd done, I knew I had only one chance to prove I was lucid and sane. One narrow window.

"I don't remember anything at all."

"Oh?"

"I'm a somnambulist."

"I see," the policeman said. "You walk in your sleep?"

I nodded.

A paramedic took my blood pressure.

"And you walked from the caravan park to Keeper's Point in one night."

I scanned the moon shadows beyond the lights from the ambulance. "Certainly seems that way."

"Five kilometers? You walked five kilometers in the dark, while you were asleep?"

"More common than you might think," one of the paramedics said.

The policeman wrote in a notebook. "What's with the screaming, then?"

"Screaming?"

"We got a call from one of the locals. That's why we're here. Scared the life out of her. She thought you'd gone over the edge."

I remembered Amanda Creen. The coroner said she'd committed suicide, but she might have stepped over the rail in her sleep.

"I . . . don't . . . Sometimes I have nightmares."

"Sleepwalking *and* nightmares."

"Often go hand in hand," the paramedic explained. "Perhaps we'd better take you to the hospital and get one of the doctors to have a look at you, hey?"

"No," I snapped. "I'm fine. I have to work today."

"Where's work?" the policeman asked.

"John Barton's."

"Ha! I knew I'd seen you before. You're John's new lad. You were helping us out on the highway. Picking up pieces."

I nodded enthusiastically, but I didn't remember the face.

For a moment, they all stopped what they were doing and stared.

I'd played my get-out-of-hospital-and-jail-free card without knowing it. Somehow, working for John Barton, working with the dead and picking up the pieces, allowed me an abnormal range of "normal." Somehow, working for John justified my screaming somnambulism.

"You'll live," declared the paramedic with a smile. "I'd recommend making an appointment with your GP about the sleepwalking."

I sat up on the trolley and flipped the blanket aside. "Sorry for any inconvenience. I hope I haven't caused too much trouble."

A pause in the conversation allowed us all to hear a wave rush into the rocks below the point.

"Not at all," the policeman said. "I'll give you a ride back to town when the boys have finished with you."

The paramedic who'd taken my blood pressure jabbed a finger into my shoulder. "See your doctor."

I said I would.

The policeman led me by the elbow to the patrol car.

"I used to sleepwalk," he whispered. "When I was a kid. My mum pinned a bell to my pajamas."

"Really? Did it wake you?"

He shook his head, laughed a little. "It would wake Mum, though, and she'd stop me from hurting myself or wandering off into the night. Apparently, I made it out the door one time. Nothing like this, though. You're an Olympic champion compared with me, Aaron."

30

ARRIVED AT WORK JUST as John was opening the doors for business.

"Morning," he sang, and ran for his office. I could hear the phone ringing.

I headed for the cool-room.

"Yes, of course," I heard John say. "It is an absolute tragedy." A long silence followed.

There were no new bodies in the mortuary.

"Mr. Campbell?" John finally said, his voice croaky and re-strained. "Mr. Campbell, are you still there?"

My ears pricked up, and I held my breath.

"No, don't apologize. Just take a moment. I can wait for you if you like, or would you rather I called again . . . Of course. Hartford Street. Number sixteen. We'll be there within the hour. Not at all. Thank you, sir."

He hung up and exhaled loudly. I leaned against his door-jamb, arms crossed on my chest.

John was reclining in his chair with hands clasped behind his head, lips tight. He stared at me for so long, he could have taken an olden-days photograph. In time, he said, "You may want to sit this one out."

I prickled at the implication. I'd wrestled back the tears and sat through harrowing services. I'd collected heads and smelled the decay. I'd—

"Child," he whispered.

I swallowed hard. It made a noise.

"Five years old. He went missing yesterday afternoon. They found him in their rainwater tank."

"I'll be okay," I said.

John stared.

I held his gaze. I didn't blink, but something inside my head was overly tight. Something was stretched to the point of ir-reparable damage, and I wanted to bounce on it until it broke. Maybe that's what had happened to Mam? Maybe the rubber band that powered her memory had snapped? *Bring the child. Bring the death. Break the band. Bring the oblivion.*

Sixteen Hartford Street sparkled. Fresh paint, flowers in bloom. The sadness, like the death, was so new that there was no sign of decay. The ambulance was there. The paramedic recognized me, acknowledging me with a discreet nod. A small crowd of voyeurs stood on the street. We transferred the small, blanket-wrapped body from the ambulance gurney to ours, and left the scene without saying a word.

His eyes and skin were the palest blue. His long eyelashes had stuck together with water or tears as if he wore mascara. His lips were closed. His midnight hair hung curled and damp into his collar, a month late for a haircut. His child's fingers curled weightless around nothing. His feet were bare.

John didn't look at the child—he looked at me. He must have heard my breathing fail, sensed my rubber band snap. I felt it go. The still boy on the bench reached way into my past and undid the tightest knot.

John Barton, to his credit, didn't try to stop me and didn't say a word as I left. Well, if he did, I didn't hear him. Somehow, I made my way home and into the van. Still in my shoes and tie, I drew Mam's quilt and my knees to my chin and huddled into the corner of her bed.

I'd never been so hungry for sleep in my life, but memories wheeled around in my brain without any form or reason. The monkey had *my* remote. Voices sliced through the caravan walls in fits, blistering with anger or fear, I couldn't tell which.

The voices weren't inside my head. They were coming from van fifty-seven.

The voices poked me like sharp icicles until I had to cover my head, but the quilt didn't keep them out. I felt wired, adrenaline bubbling in my veins like a zillion coffees. One thought found purchase. It kept playing over and over in my head—I imagined the boy in the tank, the moments before his surrender. I imagined that the noises from van fifty-seven were his screams. The sounds were trapped in the tank with him. His fingers pawed at the wet plastic but could find no hold.

I'm the drowning boy. I've been drowning for years.

31

I CAN HEAR HIS VOICE NOW, *but I don't understand the words. My mother's eyes are closed, and I envy her death. He shoves me to the floor and sits heavily in a blood-spattered velvet armchair in front of me. Is it blue or black? He levels the shotgun at my head. I close my eyes and the fear is gone. It leaves like a sigh and I am free. The shell explodes and I feel it. I hear it with the soles of my feet and the pit of my belly.*

Upside-down with the taste of blood. I righted myself in a panic and saw the insides of the van glowing under moonlight. Mam's towel was on the floor beside me. My lips were sticky, my work shirt stained and damp.

There was movement in the annex, and I spun to see a figure silhouetted in the doorway, moonlight filtering green around him. A stocky form, a man with a fat shadow in his hands, his head a smooth dome. As he ripped the sliding door open and ran, I saw that the shadow was a gun. Outside, the moon was so bright that I saw his eyes glint as he flicked a glance over his shoulder. I saw swirled patterns of tattoo ink on the pale skin of his head.

I stepped to the sliding door and watched the figure running in a crouch toward the road. Lights flicked on in van fifty-seven, and the air instantly split with a scream of absolute horror. It tore through me like the sound of fingernails on a blackboard. I ran.

The scream had come from Candy. She was naked, on her knees on the floor of their annex, her saggy breasts covered in blood. Westy's head, cradled in her lap, was the wrong shape. Part of it had been blown away. Candy patted his cheek with a shaking hand and called his name.

"Somebody help me!" she screamed, toothless, at the ceiling. Through her tears, she saw me in the doorway.

"No!" she bawled. She hugged her son's head tighter. "Get away from me!"

I heard footsteps on the gravel and with a flash of insight, ran for the phone.

"Hey!" shouted a man. "Stop!"

I glanced over my shoulder, saw the shadow of the man who'd called, and ran harder. I could explain—

My head exploded—all strobe lights and pain—and I fell to the ground. Instantly, a heavy knee was in my back, and my lips dragged on the gravel.

"I might have known," Tony Long growled. He grabbed my arms and pinned them up behind my back. "Nerida! Nerida? Call the cops. I knew this was going to happen. Just bloody *knew* it."

The pain radiated from my right cheek. I squirmed enough to realize I could flip Tony Long off my back, but there were people in robes everywhere. I didn't know so many slippers lived in the park. From where my head was pinned, I could see them filing to the door of Westy's van, following the grief-stricken howling of his mother to its source. They variously swore and covered their mouths at what they saw. Some watched from a safe distance. Nobody went inside.

Slippers scurried on the gravel. "The police are on their way."

"Thank God for that," Tony Long said. "Don't go over there, love. Don't."

"Why not?" Nerida Long said, scuffing past my face and heading for the light of the annex.

I watched her face contort. I watched her squeal. I watched her turn away and vomit on the grass.

Come on, Nerida, I thought, *show a bit of stomach.*

The police arrived. Tony Long shifted his weight and grabbed my hair.

"This is the bloke," he yelled. "Got him. He was making a run for it. Got him." He swapped knees and ground my face into the path in some sort of feeble victory dance.

Cool metal rasped around my wrists, and I was lifted to my feet.

I didn't feel safe until I'd been locked in the back of the divisional van. And I didn't stop shaking until the moonlight became the blinding glare of caged fluorescent tubes in the cell at the station. They took the handcuffs. They took my shoes, my bloodstained tie, and my belt. The front of my shirt bore an inkblot of crimson. I didn't breathe a full breath until they'd left and latched the door.

I was there for hours. Shadows swept past the door, and

occasionally they'd stop and peer in. I realized near dawn that it was the same woman checking on me, making her rounds like a nurse. Making sure I hadn't trashed the cell or done damage to myself. I could hear a faint bird song when the door rattled, and she finally came inside.

"Morning, Aaron."

She had a plastic bowl with warm water and a tattered white cloth. She wore blue surgical gloves.

"It *is* Aaron, isn't it?"

I couldn't remember her face. Constable Nadine Price, her nametag said. The one whose jacket I'd borrowed when they found me near the café.

"Thought I'd give you a chance to tidy yourself up before they question you. Okay?"

She wet the cloth and handed it to me. The smell of disinfectant ripped up my nose, and I coughed.

"Sorry about that. Hospital strength."

I wiped the crust from my upper lip, dragged the cloth over my neck and collar, and handed it back to her.

She rinsed it and gave it back. "There's blood on your cheek."

I rasped it across my face and winced. The gravel had broken the skin. I dabbed at my cheek, and the cloth came away stained. I held it in place and felt the warmth in the bone.

"Need a swab for forensics, I'm afraid," she said.

A scrape from inside my mouth, a dab from my bleeding face.

"Is there anyone you'd like to call? Let them know where you are?" She waited a while, staring.

I handed her the cloth and she left.

I curled into a ball on the vinyl mattress on the floor. I rocked, ever so slightly.

Rock the baby.

But the baby will never sleep.

The door to my cell clattered, and I remembered where I was and the reason I was there. Panic locked in my throat as two large and unfamiliar men carrying plastic chairs entered the room. I stood, and the larger of the two instructed me to sit. I crossed my legs on the mat like a school kid. They came armed with pens, clipboards, and a tape recorder. The door closed, and my body started rocking of its own accord, barely moving, to the rhythm of my pulse.

The big guy started the tape, checked his watch, and told the microphone the time and date.

"Can you state your name, please?" he asked his clipboard.

When I didn't respond, he looked at me. Even his eyebrows—narrow, stern caterpillars—seemed intimidating.

"Name?" the other guy said.

I opened my mouth to speak, but nothing came out.

"Can ... you ... tell ... us ... your ... name?" he said, louder.

"No use, Doug," the big man said, standing. "I'll get someone from special services down."

He rapped on the glass in the cell door, and it was opened from the other side.

"That was quick!" a voice said. The two men stepped into the hallway.

"I don't get it," Doug said as he left. "Is it some sort of joke?"

"Hey?"

"How come we're always dumped with the retards?" The door closed on their laughter.

Not a retard, sir. Just a broken unit. With nowhere to hide.

32

MY EARS ARE RINGING. *Always ringing. My exposed skin is spattered with remains, and I squeeze my eyes shut. I'm frightened of what I won't see. When the rain of dreck subsides, I take stock of my limbs and finally look around. David is in the velvet chair, but he has turned the gun on himself. His head has become a messy flower on the pitted wall.*

I was panting like a dog, a warm hand on my shoulder.

"Steady, Aaron. It's okay. It's me, John."

My eyes were wide but fuzzy-blind for several long seconds; and then I saw him in his suit and tie, his brow creased with concern.

I sighed when I recognized him, squeezed the hand on my shoulder.

"You okay?" he asked.

I nodded.

He helped me to my feet. "Can you walk?"

I hopped a few steps, my legs sleep-dead and awkward.

"Let's get you home," he murmured.

The cell door opened, and the policeman let us pass.

Nobody tried to stop us as I walked through the station in my socks, into the car park, and into the passenger seat of the silver Mercedes.

"Told you drugs were no good," mumbled Skye from the back seat.

I looked over my shoulder at her in her school uniform, the tips of her shower-wet plaits like paintbrushes. She had her arms crossed over her chest and a scowl on her face.

I smiled. I'd been remembered. "How did you find me?" I asked.

"Nadine Price is an old family friend," John said. "She called after she'd finished work this morning. Said you were in . . . in a bit of trouble."

"What did you do?" Skye asked.

"Nothing," I said.

The car fell quiet and remained that way until we pulled up at the caravan park. A fire truck blocked the entrance. They were packing up hoses. A helmeted fireman came to John's window.

"Have to walk from here," he said. "The truck will be another ten minutes or so."

John thanked him.

I undid my seat belt.

John grabbed my arm and looked me in the eye, hard.

"You're on bail," he said. "I gave them my assurance you'd stay in town."

I swallowed.

"Have you got a clean shirt? Where's your tie?"

I felt my collar. "The police took it."

"Grab what you need. You can get changed at our place." He dropped my arm and I ran.

A pall of dirty smoke hung in the campground.

The van at fifty-seven had been cordoned off with blue and white tape. The door was shut. The lights were out.

Around the corner, Mam's van was gone. In its place was a slumped and charred pile of melted aluminum and tiny cubes of glass. A blackened annex wall had fallen over the steel skeleton of Mam's armchair, and the whole pile that had once been my home hissed faintly.

Nothing had been saved. Nothing was salvageable in that distorted pile. Everything had gone, and I felt one step closer to freedom. One step closer to death.

"Hey!"

I turned to see Tony Long running toward me.

"What the hell are you doing here?"

I ran hard and circled back to the Bartons' car. I slammed the door.

"Drive!" I howled.

The rear wheels coughed on the gravel, and we were gone.

"What was that all about? Where are your clothes?"

I caught my breath. "The van's gone. Burned to the ground."

"What?"

"Who were you running from?" Skye asked. "The cops?"

"No, Tony Long. The park manager."

John looked at me, puzzled. "Are you okay?"

"Sorry, yes, I'm fine. It's a long story."

The car fell quiet again, but the air fizzed with expectation. The Bartons were waiting for the story.

"The sound of a shotgun woke me last night. I don't know what time. I'd fallen out of bed and . . . I don't know. My nose had bled. I saw the shape of somebody in the annex. A bald guy with tattoos on his head. He had a gun. He ran. That's when I heard the screaming. Somebody had shot the guy in number fifty-seven. Blown half his head away. I ran for the phone at the kiosk, but Tony Long thought I was running from the crime, and he decked me. Held me to the ground until the police arrived."

They held their breath. I held mine. It felt like the longest story I'd ever told. Ever. I wasn't used to the sound of my own voice.

"Did you do it?" John asked.

"No! Of course not. I don't think so. I couldn't have done it. I don't have a gun."

I said those words, and some part of me knew them to be true, but the doubt in John Barton's voice shook my own confidence. I *could* have killed Westy. The rage he spawned in me was monstrous. All curved white teeth and sickle claws. If that beast broke loose in my sleep, anything would be possible. Anything could happen and I wouldn't know. I *could* have killed Westy.

"You're shaking," Skye said.

I sat on my hands until John had parked the car in his garage.

Mrs. Barton had tears in her eyes. She hugged my head,

briefly and awkwardly. I was shuffled into Skye's bathroom, and Skye was shuffled off to school. I showered and changed into one of John's T-shirts and a pair of his tracksuit pants—there was room for two at the waist, and they were midcalf length. Slippers on my feet. The cut on my cheek was too tender to shave, so the overall impression in the mirror was of an escapee or homeless person.

Mrs. Barton chuckled and covered her mouth when she noticed the pants.

"I'll wear my coveralls."

"Of course," she said. "Should have thought of that myself."

John set me to work building caskets. I was safe from the eyes of the public and free to wrestle with my demon thoughts. Several times I looked up to find him watching me. Reading me. Studying me. I hoped he'd find the answer and let me know.

I couldn't shirk the task of assembling the smallest box. I knew the child was in the mortuary, but I wasn't hiding from the body, either. I knew the dead boy didn't care, but I was sorry for the way I'd reacted. I took extra care in preparing his casket. John had set his features, and I lifted him myself, felt his tiny limbs hang, and laid him in state.

"Nice work," John whispered, his eyes glossy.

"Why do you do this for me?" I asked.

John sniffed. "What?"

"Why do you keep picking me up when I fall down? Why are you so generous? How can you trust me the way you do?"

He dabbed his eyes and left the cool-room. "I don't know, Aaron. Maybe I'm a gullible fool."

After crustless sandwiches and pumpkin soup, John drove me to town, and I shopped for toiletries and clothes—more white shirts, a tracksuit, and boxer shorts bright enough to make an undertaker proud. He smiled when he saw them and offered to pay. When I refused, he stuffed a wad of cash in my hand.

"Payday," he said.

I left the shop with a pocket full of change and my dignity intact.

"You missed your license test yesterday," he said on the way home.

"I'm . . . I'm sorry about that. Sorry about how I reacted."

He lifted a shoulder. "You're here. You did what you needed to do."

Shot an irritating neighbor? Spent a night in the clink? Burned my home down?

"I don't know what you have planned for this evening, but you are welcome to stay in the spare room."

I showed him my palm. "You're doing it again! Why? What have I done to deserve this kindness?"

He smiled. "Is that a yes or a no?"

I snorted and shook my head. "It's a yes. Thank you."

He nodded, and the van went quiet except for my shopping bags rustling at my feet.

"There's no simple answer," John said to the windscreen. "You understand death."

He looked at my eyes. "You know death and it disturbs you, yet you look it in the face. I've seen you run from it only to find your balance and come back for more. They're the hallmarks of someone who values life. If you didn't feel the death or it . . . fascinated you . . . I'd be concerned."

My face burned. I thought about Amanda Creen's hair. I thought about Taylor.

"I may yet be proven wrong, but right here, right now, I think you're worth the effort."

I bowed my head and let the tears flow. They tickled the sides of my nose and crashed onto the plastic bags.

"Do you snore?" Skye asked at the dinner table. "You snore, and I'll come in and pour a bucket of ice on your head."

Mrs. Barton leveled a finger at her daughter. "You'll do no such thing. You go anywhere near Aaron, and you'll find yourself sleeping in the mortuary. Do you understand?"

"If he snores, Aaron can sleep with the dead," Skye mumbled.

"I don't think I snore," I said. "Sorry in advance if I do."

"What about your nightmares?" Skye said.

Her father shushed her.

"And your sleepwalking! Dad, have you got any rope?"

"Enough!" John snapped. "Leave the poor lad alone, Skye. We'll sort it out. You don't need to worry about anything. You hear a noise, you go back to sleep, okay?"

"Not likely," she muttered.

I could tell from the look on John's face that he was wondering what he had done, what he had brought into his home.

"Thank you," I said, for the hundredth time. "I'm sorry to turn your world upside-down like this. I'll find a place to stay tomorrow."

"Turn *our* world upside-down?" Mrs. Barton blurted. "Have

a look at what's left of *your* world. It's no trouble at all. Stay as long as you need. You won't be sitting idle, mind you. Don't be surprised if Mr. Barton wakes you in the middle of the night to go and fetch a body."

I flashed a smile. I hoped he would wake me but doubted it. I liked the idea of collecting the dead in the dark. Easy to be discreet after nightfall. That would almost make us an emergency service. The ambulance would whisk away the living; we'd whisk away the rest. The kernel of dread in my guts was fed by Skye's fears. What if I did wake? What if I did scream? What if I couldn't sit idle even in my sleep?

33

LAY ON THE CLEAN LINEN in the spare bedroom, too frightened to sleep, too frightened to let myself go. Dressed in a scratchy new T-shirt and lurid boxer shorts, I rolled and breathed and tried to hide from the insomniac chatter in my head.

I could have killed Dale West. Would have killed him in another place or another time where death was more common and expected. I could sleepwalk, so why not sleep *maim,* sleep *strangle,* or sleep *shoot*? Perhaps jail would be the safest place for me. Maybe a few years behind bars was all I needed to grow out of this madness. Like a bed wetter with a plastic sheet, I fantasized about a night of uninterrupted sleep.

"Aaron?"

I sat up, my heart pitching. The moonlight revealed Skye standing there in her pajamas.

"What? What do you want?"

"Nothing," she whispered. "I heard you wriggling around. Having trouble sleeping?"

"No," I hissed. "I'm fine. Go back to bed."

"Your nightmare really happened, didn't it? It's the same every time, I know it."

I sighed and clicked my lips like Mam in her sleep.

She dragged a blanket from the box at the end of the bed, draped it over her shoulders, and settled on the chair in the corner.

"Go to bed, Skye. If your mother catches you in here, you'll—"

"Who cares?"

"*I* care!" I hissed. "I'm enough of a burden on your parents without keeping you up all night."

"My nightmares are almost exactly the same," she said aloud.

"Shhh!"

"I go into his bedroom and he's cold. I wake myself trying to wake him up. When I was little, I used to run into their room and climb between them. Now I'm okay as long as I can hear them snoring. Hearing my dad trying to sniff his nose inside out puts me back to sleep. You can snore if you want to. I don't mind. Really."

"Thank you," I said. "Go to bed."

"You're not the boss of me. I'm the boss of you, remember?"

Perhaps I could *pretend* I was asleep when I strangled her. I slumped onto my pillow and dragged the quilt over my head, but she didn't leave, just hummed and tapped a foot on the floor.

I rolled onto my back and sighed at the ceiling. With Skye in the chair in the corner, I felt as if I was on a psychologist's couch. A twelve-year-old psychologist.

"Same room," I said. "Same scene, but every time it's another chapter or a slightly different angle."

"I remember that much. And?" She prompted, barely leaving enough time for a breath.

"And, yes, I know the room."

"And?"

"And there's a woman in the bed. She's not quite dead in the beginning, but she's dying from a bullet wound in her stomach. The man who shot her is standing in the doorway with a gun, smoking."

"Oh my God," she whispered.

I was leaking words. I couldn't stop.

"The man is shouting at me, but I can't understand what he's saying. He drags me by the hair to the pillow, and I watch the woman die."

"Jesus."

"He pushes me to my knees on the floor and points the gun at my head. I close my eyes, and I know I'm going to die, but I don't care. The gun goes off."

She was silent then. Silent except for the little animal breaths whistling in and out of her nose.

"When I open my eyes again, the man has blown his own head off."

Skye held her breath. "Is any of it . . . real?"

"Of course," I said. "It's all real. Everything."

Some sort of emotional depth charge went off in my belly, and I howled like a wild dog. Howled until all my air was gone and I was drowning.

Of course it was real. Every little detail. I'd lived it a million times but never told the story. Never packaged it in words and mailed it to the world.

The light flicked on, but I couldn't stop. Skye had disappeared, and her father was there, rumple haired and tying his bathrobe. He sat on the bed and held my hand.

"It's okay, Aaron. Just a dream, mate. Hush!"

"It wasn't a dream," I bawled. "It was never a dream."

He patted my chest. "Shhh."

I squeezed his fingers, and he squeezed back. I felt the blundering intimacy of the moment and tried to pull away.

John held tight. "Tell me what happened," he whispered.

I sniffed and swallowed, wiped my face on my sleeve. He helped me sit up.

"Canada. When I was five. My father killed my mother," I said, and gagged.

John drew a breath, but he held on.

"He shot her in the guts in her bed."

John nodded as if nothing was new.

"He made me watch her die and then turned the gun on himself."

John made a noise, an involuntary whimper.

"I wish he'd killed me, too."

"Hush," John said. "He didn't. By some miracle you're still here. What happened after that?"

I breathed in. I breathed out.

"Then Mam came and got me. I've been with her here ever since, and she's lived with the knowledge that her only son killed his wife and himself. Left her with this . . . broken child. She gave up her life for me. She taught me everything. Did everything for me. She was a professor at university. She was so smart. It drove her around the bend. I'm the reason she's in the hospital."

"Hang on a minute," John said. "She's sick, Aaron, but you can't blame yourself for that. Nothing you did or didn't do contributed to Mam's illness. Do you hear me?"

I wiped my eyes.

"Hear me?" he said again.

"Yes, I hear you."

"Now, I have a confession to make to you. I knew Mam's story through a mutual friend, and I made the connection after I hired you."

I stiffened. The running man who had found me on the beach. The paramedic guy from the university, I was sure of it. Suddenly John's kindness seemed contrived. Suddenly John was a do-gooder, and I was his latest case. "I don't need your sympathy. I don't need anybody's sympathy."

"Stop it!" he growled. He pushed at my chest.

I struggled to get free, but he pinned me to the headboard. His strength surprised me.

He watched my eyes until I stopped fighting.

"I lost a son," he said.

I blinked.

"Died from a brain tumor. Went to sleep and didn't wake up eight years ago. Skye found him. She was shaking him and peeling back his eyelids when I came in."

"I'm sorry," I said.

"I don't want you to be sorry," he said. "All I wanted to say was that death is never going to go away. We deal with it the best way we can. We deal with it, and we get on with living. Me, I started a business and surrounded myself with the dead and the grieving. I'm not sure it was entirely the healthiest way to deal with it, but here I am. I love what I do."

That much was obvious. I felt a moment's envy for his courage. His son had died, and he had turned it into a career. A strong, successful, healthy career. To some, it might seem morbid, but to me he was being brave. I wished that courage came in pill form—then I'd live out Skye's fantasy and become a drug addict.

I'd stopped crying. I filled my lungs, and corners of my being that hadn't tasted air in a decade were refreshed. My history was essentially the same, but something felt different.

John tousled my hair. "Sleep. There's work to do in the morning."

For the first time in a very long while, I did.

34

THERE'S BANGING AT THE DOOR. *I can hear a man shouting, a bump and a crunch, and then the man is wide-eyed in front of me. He's a policeman with his hat in his hand. He looks at the bodies of my mother and my father and hurries away to vomit in the other room. When he returns, he kneels before me with his big warm hand on my shoulder.*

"What's your name, little man?" he asks, his voice tremulous.

"Aaron David Rowe," I say.

He wipes my brow with his fingers. "Well, Aaron, how would you like to come with me?"

His paw swallows mine, and he leads me into the hall. There are people looking at us from the cracks of doors. Their faces shout fear, but nobody says a thing. The doors close like clams as we pass.

I woke when Mrs. Barton slid the curtains open.

"Afternoon, Aaron. Hope this isn't going to be a regular matinee show because I will tire of it very quickly."

I rubbed my eyes. "Sorry. First and last time," I said.

She smiled. "You may want to get dressed. You have visitors of the official kind."

Panicking, I dragged tracksuit pants over my boxer shorts and patted my hair flat.

Constable Nadine Price and the other woman who'd helped me home from the café—Kim—sat in the lounge. Their teacups and cake plates were half empty. They stood when I entered.

"Hi, Aaron," Constable Nadine Price said.

I mumbled hello.

"No need to be scared, mate," Constable Kim said. "This is just an informal little chat."

"Sit down, Aaron, for goodness' sake," Mrs. Barton said. "They've been fed; they won't eat you."

I took a seat, and Mrs. Barton poured me a cup of tea and put a slice of sponge cake on a plate. Cake for breakfast? The day was about to get stranger.

"Now, could you tell us what happened at the caravan park the other day?"

"I should go," Mrs. Barton said.

"Please stay," I said. "If it's okay with . . ."

"Of course," Constable Nadine Price said. "Be aware, Aaron, that we'll take note of what you say, and we might use it in court."

I thought about that for a few long seconds. They knew about my sleepwalking—had seen it firsthand. I told them my version of events, and they didn't interrupt. Just the facts. They didn't put me in cuffs when I was done, but they kept asking questions.

"So you have no memory of what happens when you sleep-walk?"

"No," I said.

"So you could have had a hand in the murder of Dale West and not remember it?"

Mrs. Barton squirmed in her seat.

"Yes," I said. "I could have."

"Tell us more about the man you saw in the annex of your van when you woke up."

I described his silhouette and the small details the moon-light had revealed—the bald head and tattoos. The gun.

Constable Kim spread out a sheaf of mug shots on the cof-fee table. "Is he there anywhere?"

Third from the left. Spirals on top of his head. The two constables smiled.

"I think we're about done for today, Aaron. Thank you for your time."

"What?" I said. "What happens now?"

"Well," Constable Nadine Price said. "We may need you to stand up in court and identify the man you saw in your van, so don't go on any overseas trips without letting us know."

"I don't have to go to jail?"

She smiled kindly. "Probably not."

Constable Kim stood and collected her hat. "Forensics says the blood on your tie was yours and yours only. There were two other people who saw Mr. Gwynne at the van arguing with Mr. West, and when we paid Mr. Gwynne a visit later that morning, there was a shotgun in the boot of his car."

"Not exactly a criminal mastermind," Constable Nadine Price said.

"And not the sort of fellow you want to owe money to," Constable Kim added.

"Twenty-five thousand dollars, so they say."

Westy had been in deep.

35

I SAT WITH THE BARTONS around the television on Saturday night, watching *The Simpsons,* feeling like a spare wheel, and trying not to laugh too loudly. I made a cup of tea for Mrs. Barton. I made a hot chocolate for Skye—with one white marshmallow.

"Thank you, Robot," she whispered.

"My absolute pleasure," I whispered back.

She looked at me strangely.

"What?" I asked. "Hot chocolate not perfect?"

"It's not that," she said. "I'm going to have to think up a new nickname for you."

"Oh?"

"You don't sound like a robot anymore," she said with a grin.

John Barton was on his second beer—his limit, he said, because he was always on call—and made a confession.

"Remember that song by Queen? 'Another One Bites the Dust'?"

"Of course," I said.

"Sometimes, when the phone rings and they tell me the sad

news, I hear that song in my head. 'Bamp bamp bamp bamp, another one bites the dust.'"

"John Kevin Barton!" his wife scolded. "You are a disgrace! Don't tell the boy that!"

"'Bamp bamp bamp bamp' . . . ouch!"

Mrs. Barton slapped him. It would have seemed violent if you hadn't seen her smile.

I guess we deal with death the best way we can.

I lay awake for a full minute that night before I nodded off. I slept like a tree, without a dream. I woke with a dribble patch on my pillowcase and looked at it with a certain sense of pride. I'd barely moved.

Was it really that simple? Were my nighttime horrors so easily tamed? I knew the dream was real; the five-year-old me had been living it forever. It had shaped and colored my world and would continue to do so as long as I lived, but it was no longer driving the bus. And my sleepwalking? If it happened again, I'd see a doctor. It was possible, I thought, that I'd been running from the dream all along.

At eleven o'clock that morning, someone from the hospital called to say there was a pickup.

My heart pounded in my throat as I eavesdropped.

"Well, Aaron. Time to earn your keep," John said.

We were in the van, with the garage door opening, when John patted my hand.

"Mam's fine," he said. "But you can visit her while I do the paperwork if you like."

The nurse on duty in Finch Ward let me through the locked door and walked me to Mam's room.

Mam was tucked in her bed, apparently asleep. I planted a kiss on her slack cheek.

Her eyes snapped open, and she beamed a smile that made me laugh out loud. She opened her arms to me. "Here he is!"

I took her hug for all it was worth.

36

AT FOUR FORTY-FIVE on Monday afternoon, I walked from the license testing office with a piece of yellow paper held triumphantly above my head. John stood beside the silver Mercedes and clapped. He shook my hand and patted my back. There were L-plates already in place—front and rear. He opened the driver's door and ushered me inside.

"I'm not sure I'm ready for—"

"No time like the present," he said. "Take it easy. You'll be fine."

I sat and checked the mirrors. I saw Skye in the back seat, stern faced.

"Should I be wearing a helmet?" she asked.

I snorted.

"Dad, are there airbags in the back here?" she yelled. "I want an airbag!"

"Hush, child," John said as he sat. "Put your head between your knees. Hold tight. You'll be okay."

He looked across at me and smiled. "Home, James."

I nodded and started the car.

We'd all be okay.